"Oh, look, there they are," Enid said, pointing to the area near the back of the Patman Mansion.

The guys were standing in a huddle with Christian in the middle. He looked so vulnerable standing there alone, surrounded by the Sweet Valley High and Palisades High gangs. But at least he was all right.

"I see Christian," Elizabeth said. "But where's Todd?"

"He's standing near the bushes," Enid said.

"Oh yes, I see him." Elizabeth slumped back in the car seat and exhaled a long, shaky breath. "I was so scared we'd find a disaster here, but it looks like they're finally talking."

"Guess the guys are smarter than we thought," Enid said with a wry smile.

Jessica sniffed. "Yeah. Maybe they've decided to grow up at last." She popped open the glove box and rummaged through the contents for any makeup odds and ends she could find. "I just want to get Christian out of there and leave. This whole situation has been one big nightmare and I'm sick of—" Suddenly Elizabeth and Enid screamed.

"What—" Jessica looked up and gasped in horror. A huge fight had broken out, as instantaneous as a flash of lightning and worse than anything she had ever imagined.

SWEET VALLEY High®

A KISS BEFORE DYING

Written by
Kate William

Created by
FRANCINE PASCAL

BANTAM BOOKS
NEW YORK • TORONTO • LONDON • SYDNEY • AUCKLAND

RL 6, age 12 and up

A KISS BEFORE DYING
A Bantam Book / March 1996

Sweet Valley High® *is a registered trademark of Francine Pascal*
Conceived by Francine Pascal
Produced by Daniel Weiss Associates, Inc.
33 West 17th Street
New York, NY 10011
Cover art by Bruce Emmett

ISBN: 0-553-56640-7

Published simultaneously in the United States and Canada

Bantam Books are published by Bantam Books, a division of Bantam
Doubleday Dell Publishing Group, Inc. Its trademark, consisting of the
words "Bantam Books" and the portrayal of a rooster, is Registered in U.S.
Patent and Trademark Office and in other countries. Marca Registrada.
Bantam Books, 1540 Broadway, New York, New York 10036.

PRINTED IN THE UNITED STATES OF AMERICA

OPM   0 9 8 7 6 5 4 3 2 1

To Cassity Nicole Phillips

Chapter 1

Elizabeth Wakefield was trapped in a nightmare of flashing lights, police sirens, and angry shouting. All around her, guys with bruises and bloodstained faces were being handcuffed and pushed into police cars. Her own boyfriend, Todd Wilkins, had been arrested and was on his way to jail. Right next to her, a policeman's radio switched on, startling her with a sudden burst of crackling static.

Elizabeth wrapped her green sweater tighter around herself, overlapping its front edges, and then folded her arms over her chest, as if to protect herself from the chaos. Someone bumped her from behind. She turned to see a tall, scowling police officer pushing two handcuffed guys ahead of him, one whose neck was bleeding profusely.

A few yards away, Bruce Patman was lying face-down on the ground as a female officer stood over him, reading him his rights. Elizabeth had known Bruce since childhood. He did have a hot temper and a reckless side, but it shocked her to see him treated like a dangerous criminal.

Elizabeth had called the police because she suspected something terrible was going to happen tonight. And she had been right. It'd been every bit as terrible as she'd feared.

Enid Rollins, her best friend, stepped up beside her. "This is so awful," Enid said, a look of horror on her face. "How could an argument over a football game escalate into an all-out riot?"

"It's unbelievable, isn't it? I don't think Todd is ever going to forgive me for calling the police."

"I'm sure Todd didn't mean what he said to you, Liz."

"Didn't he?" Elizabeth whispered, overcome with a feeling of sadness. She had offered to go to the police station to help him, but Todd wanted nothing to do with her. His parting words as the police officers had pushed him into the backseat of the cruiser echoed in her mind: *Don't do me any favors!* Elizabeth exhaled a shaky breath, a dark heaviness squeezing at her chest. "I don't know what to believe anymore."

"He'll calm down soon enough," Enid mumbled.

Elizabeth wasn't convinced, but she appreciated the reassuring gesture anyway. She knew Enid was trying to be supportive.

How *could* an argument over a football game turn into this? Elizabeth wondered. A few weeks ago, their school's football team, the Sweet Valley High Gladiators, had lost a game against the Palisades High Pumas, who had played dirty. Since then, the guys of both schools had been locked in a vicious rivalry, with aggression and retaliation bouncing back and forth between them like Ping-Pong balls.

Tonight, the guys from Palisades had tricked the SVH class clown, Winston Egbert, into driving out to an abandoned warehouse on the outskirts of Sweet Valley. The guys from SVH had learned of the deception and rushed to Winston's rescue—but not before Winston had been seriously beaten.

Elizabeth, Enid, and a few other girls from Sweet Valley had arrived at the warehouse a short time later to find a battle raging like a scene from a cheap adventure movie—guys punching, shoving, brandishing sticks, staggering, blood dripping from their noses and cracked lips. Elizabeth shuddered, remembering. She would never have imagined Todd being capable of violence. But tonight she had seen a side of him that terrified her—a dark, vicious animal had replaced the sweet, gentle guy she loved.

"I'm going to go look for Maria and Winston,"

Enid said, breaking into Elizabeth's thoughts. "Will you be all right?"

Elizabeth nodded. "Go ahead. I'll catch up with you guys in a minute. I want to look for Jessica. I thought I saw her standing in the shadows on the other side of the building a little while ago."

Enid walked away without making a disparaging comment at the mention of Jessica's name, for which Elizabeth was grateful. It wasn't any secret that Enid and Jessica didn't like each other. Enid considered Jessica to be shallow and self-centered, and in some ways the labels fit. Jessica and Elizabeth were identical twins, but only in appearance. Their personalities were miles apart. Unlike her sister, Elizabeth was a conscientious student and set high goals for herself. Although she and Jessica were only in their junior year of high school, Elizabeth already knew that she wanted to be a professional writer someday. She was actively involved in her school's newspaper, *The Oracle*, as a reporter and as the writer of a weekly column. During her free time, Elizabeth enjoyed reading poetry, watching old movies, hanging out with Enid, or going on quiet, romantic dates with Todd.

Jessica lived for the moment. The most important goal in her life was having fun, which for her meant shopping, dressing up, partying, flirting, and competing for attention. And Jessica thought Enid was the most pathetic nerd she'd ever met and couldn't understand why Elizabeth allowed herself to be seen with such a loser.

Even under normal conditions, Elizabeth found Enid and Jessica's attitude toward each other to be somewhat irritating. But tonight, with so much free-floating hostility already in the air, Elizabeth couldn't bear to deal with personality conflicts as well.

While Jessica took life to be one great adventure, Elizabeth hung back, giving serious consideration to her actions. Although she had been born only four minutes before Jessica, Elizabeth was clearly the older sister. The job seemed to require a certain amount of worrying about Jessica, who rarely gave a thought to caution or common sense. Elizabeth had saved Jessica from more tight spots than she could count.

Jessica had been acting mysterious lately and Elizabeth knew that was a bad sign. Something was up with her younger sister and that could only mean trouble.

Lila Fowler and Amy Sutton, two of Jessica's best friends, were sitting on the hood of Lila's green Triumph, which was parked across the street. Elizabeth crossed the narrow gravel road and walked over to them.

Lila, Amy, Elizabeth, Enid, and Maria Santelli had rushed to the scene that evening in a desperate attempt to stop the violence. They'd all been at the Dairi Burger, a popular hangout in Sweet Valley, when they'd heard the news that Winston had been trapped by the Palisades guys.

Lila and Amy had spread a Persian rug over the car, probably so that Lila wouldn't soil her designer silk skirt. They appeared to be watching the goings-on with detached interest, as if they had the best seats at a sporting event.

"Have you seen Jessica?" Elizabeth asked.

"Yes, she was standing right there," Lila said. Her gold bracelet sparkled as she pointed to a grassy spot a few yards up the street. "We called her, but she ignored us," she added, her voice bitter. "Jessica has been acting so weird lately. I'm getting sick of it."

Amy's slate gray eyes flashed with anger. "So am I," she said. "Who does Jessica think she is, anyway?"

"Where did she go?" Elizabeth asked, ignoring their commentary.

"She took off in a blue Volkswagen bus," Amy said. "I have no idea who she was with. I couldn't see the driver and I didn't recognize the vehicle."

Elizabeth felt a gnawing urgency growing inside her. "About how long ago was it?"

Lila and Amy looked at each other and shrugged. "I don't know," Lila answered, "twenty minutes, maybe."

"That's about right," Amy agreed. "But I still

can't believe she just took off without saying one word to us. Wait till I see her. This mystery act of hers is starting to get on my nerves."

"If she comes back, tell her I'm looking for her," Elizabeth said, wishing desperately that she knew where Jessica was. The hopeful thought that she might already be safe at home occurred to Elizabeth. But years of experience warned her that it was more likely Jessica had gotten herself into another one of her infamous jams.

"Okay, but how long do we have to stay here?" Amy said impatiently. "The action seems to be dying down and I'd like to leave soon."

Amy's callous remark annoyed Elizabeth, and Lila too, it seemed. She glared at Amy, then turned to Elizabeth. "The thrill is gone, I guess," Lila said sarcastically.

Gazing at the scene across the street, Elizabeth reluctantly admitted to herself that there didn't seem to be much reason to stay. Most of the cars had cleared out of the lot and only two police cruisers remained. "I guess there's nothing left to do here," Elizabeth said. Jessica was probably long gone and wouldn't be coming back. "I'll go find Enid and Maria."

Jessica Wakefield sighed contentedly as she watched the shadows move across Christian

Gorman's face as he drove. He steered the van with one hand, the other one loosely entwined with hers in the space between the bucket seats.

They'd left the scene at the abandoned warehouse nearly an hour ago. After a long, aimless drive along the California coast, they were headed back to Sweet Valley. Neither one had spoken much, but words weren't necessary between them. The touch of Christian's hand and the look in his eyes when he glanced sideways at her communicated louder than words ever could. A feeling of love swelled in her heart. She was struck with the awesome awareness of being more alive than she'd ever felt in her life.

She only wished the dark, warm cocoon of Christian's van could shelter them forever. "I never want to go back to Sweet Valley," she said, breaking the silence.

Christian's lip twitched with the hint of a smile, but he said nothing.

"I mean it," she said.

He responded with a gentle squeeze of her hand. She smiled softly and turned to gaze at the passing scenery. The ocean shimmered in the moonlight, its vastness tugging at her heart. It was the ocean that had brought her and Christian together.

Jessica had been trying to teach herself to surf for an upcoming competition that she was determined to win. Her first attempt had turned out to be a disaster. She had wiped out badly and had lost her surfboard in the process. After she'd nearly drowned, she had washed up on the shore, sputtering and coughing.

A shadow had fallen over her as she lay there feeling sorry for herself. When she'd looked up, she had seen the most incredible, gorgeous hunk standing over her with his arm around her surfboard.

Was it really only a few weeks ago? she wondered in amazement. She turned and studied Christian's movements as he downshifted for a turn. The muscles in his arms were rock-hard, she knew, and his skin was smooth and golden. It hardly seemed possible that she'd known him for such a short time.

He had offered to teach her to surf and Jessica had marveled at her luck. As they began meeting at the beach in the early hours of the morning to practice, their feelings for each other quickly deepened, blossoming into something more than either of them had expected. Jessica had never experienced anything so wonderful in her entire life.

There was just one problem. Their timing stunk.

Jessica already had a boyfriend. She'd been dating Ken Matthews, the Sweet Valley High Gladiators' football captain, for some time. She and Christian had decided not to talk about what they did and who they were away from the beach. By telling each other only a few sketchy details of their lives, it had seemed as though their relationship existed apart from their everyday world. That was how Jessica had fooled herself into believing that seeing Christian behind Ken's back wasn't quite so bad, that she hadn't been *exactly* cheating on her boyfriend. Christian had been a fantasy, a sort of "mini-vacation" from reality.

Trouble was, reality had crashed into the fantasy, like an angry tidal wave smashing against a sand castle. A feud had broken out after a football game between the Sweet Valley High Gladiators and a rival team from a nearby town, the Palisades Pumas. Jessica and the other SVH cheerleaders had been horrified at the dirty tricks the Pumas used to beat the Gladiators. Several key members of the Sweet Valley High team had suffered injuries and in the final seconds of the game, the Pumas' quarterback had kneed Ken in the stomach, knocking the wind out of him as he was about to make what could have been a winning pass.

As Ken became more involved in the battle between SVH and Palisades, Jessica spent more time surfing with Christian. But their individual worlds, which they'd tried to keep apart, soon collided. In a cruel stroke of irony, Christian Gorman turned out to be the leader of the Palisades High gang.

Jessica closed her eyes and groaned. Only a few

hours ago, she'd been flying high with excitement in anticipation of her and Christian's first nighttime date. She'd carefully selected her outfit—a sheer and utterly sexy, gauzy green dress. She'd dabbed on her favorite perfume, *Rendezvous*, which she'd borrowed from Elizabeth. It was supposed to have been the most romantic Saturday night date of all time.

But everything had fallen apart so fast, it made her head spin. Ken had followed them to the Beachcomber Cafe, a seaside restaurant where she and Christian had planned to have an intimate, romantic candlelight dinner. Christian had been worried that something bad was going to happen that night, but Jessica had brushed aside his concerns and assured him that when they reached the restaurant, she'd give him a kiss that would drive everything else out of his mind.

She had been delivering on her promise in the foyer of the restaurant when Ken arrived. One minute, she was lost in the delicious sensations of a deep kiss—the next minute, she was looking up at Ken, his face pale with shock.

Jessica closed her eyes again, squeezing them shut. The image of Ken's stricken face tortured her. Their relationship was over, she knew that, but she cursed herself for not being up front with him from the start. Ken had been her friend before they started going together. He deserved better from her. What a mess she'd created!

"You don't think I'm serious, but I am," she said, glancing at Christian. "I really don't want to go back. Ever."

"We have to," Christian said, keeping his gaze focused on the road.

"No, we don't. Let's keep driving down the coast until we get to Mexico," she said, her words tumbling out with excitement as her mind painted a marvelous fantasy. "We'll find ourselves a secluded beach where no one will bother us. It would be so romantic, Christian. We could live in the van, surf every day, feast on tropical fruit and fresh fish . . ."

"I like fish," Christian said, playing along. "But no eels; I refuse to eat eels. And I'm allergic to shellfish."

"That's perfectly okay," she said. "You get to decide what we have for dinner."

"Really?"

"Yes, of course," she said.

He looked surprised. "That's very nice of you," he said.

"Seems only fair," she said, turning to him with a look of mock innocence. "You're the one who'll be doing all the cooking. It's my fantasy, remember."

He chuckled, a low sweet sound that she found irresistibly sexy. "You're something else, Jessica."

"Thanks, I think." She sighed wistfully, tears

gathering in her eyes. "It would be heaven if we could always be together."

Christian brought her hand to his lips and kissed her. "I wish we could," he said. "Being with you, Jessica—" He paused, taking in a deep, shaky breath. "We have to do things right," he said. "I don't want to mess up the best thing that's ever happened to me."

"I feel the same way," Jessica said. She knew the time for fantasies and games was over now. They had to return to reality and face it head-on, whether they wanted to or not.

"Come on, pal, get in there." A white-haired police officer with thick arms and enormous hands shoved Todd Wilkins into a jail cell and slammed the door shut. The metallic clanging sound echoed through Todd's head, which already hurt more than he'd thought possible.

A sharp stab of panic shot through him as he realized what was happening. He was being locked up, caged like a wild beast. The dingy gray walls and dim light seem to reflect and magnify his feeling of hopelessness. He wanted to scream, or weep—anything to stop the raging storm in his brain.

The policeman was standing on the other side of the bars, his legs spread out, his thick fists pressed against his lumpy hips. He was glaring at Todd with eyes as brown and cold as dirt. Todd suspected he had a mean streak larger than the gut that hung over his gun belt. "Now let's see if you smart boys know what's good for you," the policeman growled. "If there's any fighting—or anything that even looks, sounds, or smells like fighting, I'll get mad. And trust me boys, you don't want to make me mad."

Todd watched him walk away, wondering what he'd meant. Then he heard a sound behind him and turned around, discovering he wasn't the only one in the cell. Three other guys were in there with him. Bruce Patman was sitting on the floor in a shadowy corner, his back against the wall. Two guys from Palisades were sitting on a wooden bench on the other side of the cell. They were staring at him, whispering to each other and laughing.

Either they weren't as upset as he was or they were better at hiding it, Todd figured. He went over to Bruce and crouched down beside him.

"How're you doing, man?" Bruce whispered.

Todd shrugged, scooting over to rest his back against the wall next to Bruce. "I've been better," Todd said. He pulled his knees up and rubbed his ankle. He'd suffered an ankle injury during a basketball game and had only been out of the cast a few weeks. Once again, it struck him how ill-suited he was for all this gang warfare.

"Yeah, I've been better, too," Bruce said, his

gaze locked on the guys across the cell.

Todd recognized one of them as Greg McMullen, the Pumas' quarterback. Greg was the main instigator of the trouble, in Todd's opinion. It wasn't enough that he'd kneed Ken Matthews in the stomach during the Gladiators-Pumas football game, knocking the wind out of him; after the game, Greg and his friends had come after Ken again in the parking lot, taunting him with the name "little windbag." Then Greg had attacked him again, punching Ken in the stomach without provocation. Since then, one thing had led to another, and now here they were.

Todd wanted to believe that Sweet Valley High was right and Palisades was wrong, but what difference did it make? They'd all ended up in the same place, locked up in the same jail cell. He was ready to put an end to the fighting. Maybe if he and Bruce could talk things out with Greg and the other guy, they could work out a compromise.

Bruce had shut his eyes and he was snoring softly. Todd nudged him with an elbow to the ribs. "Wake up, Patman," he whispered urgently.

Bruce opened one eye and turned to him. "This better be good. I was having an incredible dream."

"I've been thinking," Todd began. "Maybe it's time we stop—"

"So where's your dorky friend, guys?" Greg

15

McMullen taunted, interrupting Todd's sentence. "Where's the little windbag, Ken Matthews? Guess he was too wimpy to show up tonight, huh?"

"Maybe he has a tummy ache," the other one said in a whiny voice. "He gets them often, doesn't he?"

"Can you believe he's the *captain* of the team?" Greg asked. "No wonder the Gladiators are such losers."

"Yeah!" his friend said. "Good old windbag. The cheerleaders yell, 'Go team go,' and this is Ken Matthews—" He grabbed his stomach and began making loud wheezing noises, poking fun at the way Ken had struggled for air after Greg's attack during the game. The two PH guys laughed hysterically and slapped hands, congratulating themselves.

Todd glared at them, the blood in his veins boiling hot. *Who do they think they are, talking about Ken that way?* They were nothing but slugs who made the world a scummy place. Todd's hope for peace was replaced with a blinding rage. His control snapped. He leaped toward the PH guys, barely conscious of his movements. The wooden bench toppled over with a crash. Todd pinned Greg's arms to the floor with his legs and smashed his fist into the jerk's face again and again, aware of nothing but the thudding sound of flesh hitting flesh and the scraping sensation against his knuckles.

Suddenly two strong arms gripped Todd from

16

behind and dragged him off of Greg. Todd struggled to get free, shoving and pushing his body against his captor.

"Take it easy, smart boy," a familiar voice growled in his ear. The next thing he heard was the click of handcuffs. A strong hand grabbed his shoulder and shoved him toward the door of the cell. "We'll teach you how to play rough if that's what you want, kid." Todd turned and looked into the hard, gloating eyes of the white-haired policeman.

"I told you not to make me mad," the man said, a cruel grin splitting his face.

Once again, Todd was painfully aware of everything around him. His hands were locked behind his back and a police officer was dragging him away by the collar. *I'm not a criminal!* his mind screamed. *I'm a nice kid, really. I don't belong in jail.*

The policeman opened the door of a small cell and pushed Todd inside, hard enough to knock him to the floor. "Let me know if you start itching for another fight, smart boy," he said as he leaned over Todd and removed the handcuffs. Then he locked the cell and walked away, the sound of his jeering laughter ringing through the narrow corridor.

Chapter 2

"This isn't funny, Winston. We have to get you to the hospital," Maria said, pronouncing the words clearly as if she were talking to a total idiot.

Winston could see how worried she was and he really was trying to be serious. Maria Santelli was the best girlfriend a guy could have. Winston considered himself lucky that she cared for him so much.

But he felt so confused. Where exactly were they? Bright flashing lights seemed to be swirling around his head, sirens screaming into his ears. Something had happened, he remembered. Something to do with Palisades High. He tried to think, but that only made him dizzy. Maybe his skull had been invaded by alien spiders and they were crawling around up there, destroying his thinking cells. That would explain why his brain felt as if it were wrapped in fuzzy cobwebs.

Maria pulled his arm up over her shoulders and wrapped her arm around his waist. "Come on, we have to get out of here. Can you walk, Winston?"

"Juuuur I can," he uttered in a strange, duck-quack voice. *Where did that come from?* he wondered. *An invasion of alien ducks in my throat, maybe?* He sure had a terrible taste in his mouth, come to think of it.

Enid Rollins stood next to Maria, staring at him with a look of horror. He tried to imagine what she'd think if she knew that ducks and spiders were taking him over, moving right in as if his body were a condominium complex. The idea struck him as hilariously funny and he started laughing—which sounded as if he had a kazoo stuck in his throat, making him laugh even harder.

"There he goes again," Maria said, shaking her head. "There was an ambulance here a minute ago. He refused to go near it. Can you believe that?" She turned to Winston, shaking her head. "You're so stubborn, sometimes."

He shrugged and tried to think of something to say in his defense. *Nope, the cobwebs are too thick. My brain cells are doomed!*

"I don't think he knows what's going on," Maria said.

"Do you know where you are, Winston?" Enid shouted in his face.

19

Winston nodded, and tried not to laugh again.

"Can you remember what happened?" Maria asked.

He tried. Looking around, he saw they were standing outside a brick building on a dark gravel road. There was a police car parked a few yards away from them, the source of the swirling lights. The night was cool, but he remembered he'd been sweating profusely earlier. . . .

Suddenly it all came back to him. He was supposed to meet Bruce, Todd, Ken, and the rest of the Sweet Valley High guys here in the building, which was an abandoned warehouse. But instead of finding his friends, Winston had walked into a trap. Some guys from Palisades High had tied him up and beat on him for what seemed like hours. The worst part of it was the mental torture—they kept telling him the beatings would never stop, that no one would ever find him; he'd be their prisoner forever and they'd keep him in a cage as a pet punching bag.

Winston also remembered being scared out of his mind. He'd been tempted to cry like a baby and beg for mercy, but he didn't. He'd taken it like a man. With a smug feeling of pride, he mentally congratulated himself for acting very brave.

"He might have a concussion," Enid was saying.

Maria squeezed his hand. "Don't you remember anything at all?"

"I zidn't cry." His lips were thick and rubbery, making it hard to speak. Another peal of quacking laughter bubbled out of his mouth.

Elizabeth came up to them. "Are you okay, Winston?" she asked, studying his face with a look of intense interest.

Before he could answer, Maria spoke for him. "No, he's not. We have to get him to the hospital. He needs stitches and I think his nose is broken."

"Why didn't he go to the hospital in the ambulance?" Elizabeth asked.

Maria glared accusingly at him. "Because he's too stubborn; it seems to be a common flaw among the guys lately."

"Um shtanding right here," Winston protested. "I can speak for myself." The girls kept talking to each other, ignoring him.

"Maria, why don't you drive Winston to the hospital, and Enid and I will follow you."

"Bug," Winston muttered, trying to plead with them not to leave his dear old Volkswagen Beetle behind. He tried to say more, but his lips refused to shape the words.

"What about Winston's car?" Maria asked. Winston tried to smile, but it hurt too much.

"I could drive it," Elizabeth offered.

"It's not running very well, but I know Winston loves that old tuna fish can," Maria said.

How dare you call my beautiful car a tuna fish can! Winston thought hotly.

"I'll drive right behind her," Enid said. "If Winston's car dies along the road, Elizabeth can get a ride with me."

"Excuuze me," Winston said, raising his hand. To his surprise, he couldn't hold it steady. He was trembling.

Elizabeth glanced at him, then turned back to Maria and Enid. "I think you're right. It does sound as if he broke his nose. And the side of his face looks awfully swollen."

Winston began waving his arms, trying to flag their attention. But he only managed to make himself feel dizzy. The ground began to sway and he nearly lost his balance.

Maria tightened her hold around his waist. "We'd better hurry," she said. "I think he's going to pass out any minute."

"No, Um not!" he protested.

Enid pointed to the orange Volkswagen Beetle parked by the bushes. "There's Winston's car."

"Where are his keys?" Elizabeth asked.

Maria reached around him and rummaged through the pockets of his denim jacket. "Found them," she said triumphantly, holding his key ring in the air and jiggling it like a rattle.

"Do you want us to ask Lila to call the hospital

from her car phone to let them know you're bringing him in?" Elizabeth asked.

Don't be ridiculous! Winston thought.

"That's a great idea," Maria said.

Winston watched their exchange, shaking his head. It was pointless for him to argue, he realized. There were too many of them. Once again, for the second time that evening, he was completely outnumbered. *Ganging up on Winston Egbert—what is it, the new national sport?* he wondered.

But he gave up and didn't resist as they led him to Maria's gray Camry. He may have been brave enough to withstand the PH thugs, but he knew his limits. He didn't stand a chance against these girls.

Winston wasn't the only SVH guy whose injuries required medical attention. When Elizabeth and Enid arrived at the emergency room of Sweet Valley's Joshua Fowler Memorial Hospital, a boisterous cheer rose from the crowd gathered in the waiting area. Most of the chairs along the yellow-tiled wall were occupied by guys in various degrees of distress waiting to be called to the treatment center.

Tim Nelson, the SVH Gladiators' defense linebacker, was holding an ice pack to his forehead. "Hey, Elizabeth, you should've seen Todd tonight," he said. "The guy was on the rampage like you wouldn't believe!"

"Yeah," added Ricky Ordway. "Your boyfriend turned into a warrior—a real-life Gladiator. He did us proud."

Elizabeth swallowed a feeling of disgust and walked over to the nurse's station.

"Winston Egbert is in exam room eight," the nurse on duty said. "You can't go back there just yet; only one visitor is allowed per patient and a young lady is with him right now."

"That would be Maria Santelli, his girlfriend," Elizabeth said. "Could you let her know we're here?"

"Hey, Elizabeth!" Bryce Fisherman yelled. "Any word on Todd and Bruce yet?" Bryce was a senior at SVH, with a voice loud enough to carry throughout the emergency room.

"They'd better not keep them in jail overnight," Tim said.

"Yeah!" Ricky boasted, putting up his fists. He had a nasty gash in his elbow that looked as if it needed stitches. "We'll break Todd and Bruce out of jail, just like we rescued Winston!"

The nurse turned and glared over at the guys. "Keep your voices down, please!" She turned back to Elizabeth and Enid with a look of exasperation. "It's been quite a night."

Enid rolled her eyes upward. "Yeah, tell us about it." She and Elizabeth walked over to the waiting area and sat as far away from the male cheering section as possible.

A few minutes later, Maria came out of the treatment area and joined them. Her face showed marked signs of the anguish she must have been feeling. Her complexion was unusually pale and her brown eyes were rimmed with red, as if she'd been crying.

An enthusiastic chorus of whistles erupted from the guys, hailing her arrival.

"Let's hear it for Winston, our main man!"

"He-ro, he-ro, he-ro . . ."

Maria sat next to Enid, turning her back on the guys. "They're all crazy," she said softly. "They're acting like this is just a big pep rally."

"How's Winston?" Elizabeth asked.

Maria sniffed. "He's getting x-rays right now. The PH guys really messed him up, but it'll be awhile before we know exactly how bad his injuries are." Her eyes filled with tears. "Why would anyone do this to him? Winston would never hurt anybody."

Enid put a comforting arm around Maria's shoulders. "Because just like you said, they're all crazy."

Elizabeth nodded in agreement. "Would you like to go get some coffee?" she asked. "I'm afraid *I'll* go crazy if I have to keep listening to these barbarians bragging about their great battlefield prowess."

"You two go ahead," Maria said. "I want to stay

here and wait for Winston's parents. They should be here any minute."

"Are you sure you'll be okay?" Elizabeth asked.

Maria nodded. "Bring me back some tea . . . and a fat candy bar." She gave them a watery smile. "I really need some chocolate."

"Coming right up," Enid said, jumping to her feet.

The hospital coffee shop, which was located on the other side of the building, was quite busy. Elizabeth and Enid stood in line, waiting for their turn. Two nurses in front of them were arguing the pros and cons of castile-soap enemas for surgical patients. Any other time, Elizabeth and Enid would have been on the brink of hysterical laughter, but tonight nothing could have lightened their mood.

Elizabeth couldn't stop thinking of the disastrous inter-school rivalry which was spinning faster and faster out of control. She and Enid had become friends with two girls from Palisades High that they'd met, ironically, at the very football game which had started the whole feud. Marla Daniels and Caitlin Alexander were on the staff of the *Palisades Pentagon*, the PH school newspaper. Since Elizabeth was involved with *The Oracle*, the SVH newspaper, the girls found they had much in common.

In an attempt to create something newsworthy to report, Elizabeth and her friends had come up with the idea of a SVH-PH masquerade dance. They'd held it in an old warehouse located between Sweet Valley and Palisades, which they figured would be a neutral site.

Unfortunately the rivalry between the SVH and PH guys had already begun to burn out of control. Elizabeth closed her eyes and groaned to herself as she remembered that horrible night. Instead of the fun-filled evening of music and dancing they had planned, the girls had found themselves hosting the first all-out battle of the SVH-PH War. Since then, the girls had made several attempts to bridge the animosity between their schools, but each one of their ideas ended in miserable failure.

They'd tried visiting each other's school as goodwill ambassadors, but all they got for their trouble were insults and threats. They'd published favorable articles about the other school, but their efforts had only served to inflame the growing hostility. The principals of both school had organized a joint task force to try to bring about peace, but again, the results were dismal. The war was burning hotter than ever.

Enid turned to Elizabeth. "It could take hours before we hear anything on Winston's condition. If you want to leave, you can borrow my car. I can get a ride home with Maria or Winston's parents."

Elizabeth frowned. "What makes you think I

want to leave?"

"Aren't you anxious to go to the police station and check on Todd?" Enid asked.

Elizabeth shook her head sadly. "No, I'm not. So far everything I've done to try to help the guys has backfired. I'm through with being an unwilling accomplice to this rivalry."

Enid looked at her with a bemused expression and said nothing.

"You'd really run off to Mexico with me?" Christian whispered close to Jessica's ear. The two of them were snuggled together in the back of Christian's van, her head resting comfortably on his firm, muscular shoulder.

Jessica sighed contentedly. "Anywhere," she said. "I'd go anywhere in the world with you."

He kissed her neck, then lifted his head and looked into her eyes. "You should go home," he said, his voice filled with regret. "I've kept you out much too late and—"

Jessica raised herself up on her elbow and interrupted him with a firm kiss, stopping him from saying anything more on the subject. He smiled against her lips and a deep, sexy chuckle escaped his mouth. It was game they'd been playing for hours; whenever one would mention anything about leaving, the other would kiss the words away.

When the kiss ended, Christian tucked her head back into the crook of his arm and gently stroked away a few errant strands of silky blond hair from her face. "What am I going to do with you, Jessica Wakefield?"

She snuggled closer and kissed the side of his face. "I'd say you're doing just great right now."

"I sure didn't expect things to turn out like this tonight," he said, absently running his fingers up and down her arm. "So much for our first real date."

"I know," Jessica said. Even the thrilling sensation of lying in Christian's arms couldn't wipe out the memory of this awful evening. "I wonder what was going on at the old warehouse. The fighting looked pretty bad."

"I think the SVH-PH violence has finally reached its peak."

Jessica flipped over onto her back. "There were so many police cars."

"I know. But maybe the guys have finally gotten into enough trouble with the police to make both sides come to their senses."

"Do you think that will happen?" she asked, tipping her face toward his.

Christian leaned over her and cupped her chin in his hand. "Yeah, I think it will. Then you and I can stop all the sneaking around, surfer girl. We'll be able to settle down and have an ordinary, boring, boyfriend-girlfriend relationship." He lowered his head and kissed her, a slow, sweet kiss that seemed to suggest that they had all the time in the world to enjoy each other.

Jessica hugged him tighter. Although she still felt terribly guilty about Ken, she was elated at the thought of being able to date Christian openly.

"A *boring* relationship?" she said with a joyful laugh. "With you? Never!"

Jessica slowed the Jeep to a crawl as she drove down Calico Drive and turned into the driveway of her family's split-level home. Except for the obnoxious chirping of early birds, the neighborhood was completely still. She stepped out of the Jeep and very gently pushed the door shut without making any undue noise. Then she tiptoed to the front door and slipped off her leather sandals.

Jessica didn't know precisely what time it was, but the sky was already getting light. Sunrise couldn't be too far off. If her parents woke up and discovered she'd been out all night, they'd freak. Jessica would be in more trouble than she wanted to imagine. She'd probably be grounded for the rest of her natural life or be sent away to an isolated all-girl boarding school somewhere on the other side of the world.

As quietly as a cat burglar, she pushed open the

door and crept inside. As she padded up the stairs to her room, she noticed a strip of light under the kitchen door. Her heart skipped a beat. *This is it,* she thought. *I'm dead.*

Holding her breath, she backed down the stairs and tiptoed to the kitchen door. She opened it a crack and peeked inside. "Liz," she whispered with a deep sigh of relief. "Thank goodness it's only you."

Elizabeth was sitting hunched over the kitchen table, her shoulders shaking. Jessica felt another wave of dread wash over her as she realized her sister was crying. "What's the matter?" she asked as she walked into the kitchen.

Elizabeth lifted her head and turned around. "Oh, Jessica!" she cried, jumping up and hugging her. "I was so worried," she said, sobbing. "When I got back from the hospital and you weren't here . . ." She sniffed and wiped her eyes with the sleeve of her sweater. "I imagined all sorts of horrible things that might have happened to you."

Jessica held up her hands palms forward, gesturing a halt to Elizabeth's mysterious outpouring. "Why did you go to the hospital?" she asked, trying to make sense of what her sister was saying.

"Maria, Enid, and I went with Winston to the emergency room."

"Why? What happened to him? Did he get hurt in that fight at the warehouse?"

Elizabeth nodded. "The PH guys tricked him into going to the abandoned warehouse by himself and when he got there, they ganged up on him. He was hurt badly and his nose is broken, but he'll be all right."

"I was there tonight, for a few minutes," Jessica said. "The fighting looked pretty serious."

"It was," Elizabeth said, her eyes watering again. "It was terrible. Todd and Bruce were arrested."

"Oh, no." Jessica recalled the number of police cars on the scene. "Who called the police, anyway?"

Elizabeth's lip trembled. "I did. When Todd and I found out that Winston was in danger, Todd called the rest of the SVH guys and they took off like vigilantes. I was afraid someone would get seriously hurt . . . or killed. Now Todd and Bruce are in jail and the other guys are talking about them as though they're being held as political prisoners. I'm afraid they're more bent on revenge against Palisades High than ever before."

Jessica sank into a chair, her entire body shaking as she tried to absorb what she'd just heard. With her whole heart she had wanted to believe the situation between SVH and PH was finally going to heal. But like an infected wound, it only seem to grow bigger and hotter. And now with Ken's discovery of her relationship with Christian, peace between the schools seemed hopeless.

"Elizabeth, it's even worse than you know." Jessica's hand trembled as she pushed a lock of hair behind her ear. "Remember Tuesday morning, when you came looking for me at the beach because I didn't show up at school? You know that guy I was with?"

Elizabeth's eyes narrowed. "No, I don't know him. I only know you were making out with him—and cheating on Ken."

Jessica lowered her gaze and absently traced a grain of wood in the butcher-block table with her fingernail. "I know it was wrong of me to hurt Ken. Anyway, the secret is out now. Ken walked in on us last night." She looked into Elizabeth's eyes without flinching. "I've been seeing Christian Gorman."

Elizabeth reacted as if she'd been splashed in the face with a glass of ice water. "Christian Gorman! *The* Christian Gorman? As in the gang leader of Palisades High?"

"Yes, that Christian Gorman." Then she softly added, "I'm in love with him, Liz."

Elizabeth gasped, shaking her head with a look of incredulous horror. "I really thought this whole mess couldn't get any worse. What were you thinking, going out with a gang leader?"

"I didn't know he was a gang leader when I met him. I thought he was just a cute surfer. I wanted to learn how to surf in time for the Rock TV all-state surfing competition and Christian offered to teach me. And then one thing led to another. By the time I found out who he was, it was too late. I had already fallen deeply in love."

"But he's a *gang leader*, Jessica. This is what gangs do—they go around beating up on people. Violence and gang wars are nothing new to someone like Christian Gorman."

"That's not true," Jessica said vehemently, her loyalty for Christian surging to the surface. "You have no right to say that about him. You don't know Christian. He's not like that at all. He's the sweetest, most gentle guy I've ever known."

Elizabeth looked at her with that infuriating big-sister, know-it-all gleam in her eyes. "Is that why the Palisades High gang made him their leader? Because he's so *sweet* and *gentle*?"

"I don't care if you believe me or not, but I trust Christian," Jessica said. "He wants to see the end of this stupid rivalry as much as we do."

Elizabeth reached out and squeezed her hand. "I'm sorry, Jessica. I don't have anything against the guy. I don't even know him. For that matter, I hardly know Todd anymore. I used to think *he* was so sweet and gentle, but suddenly he's acting more like a gang leader than Christian Gorman is. I guess if Todd can change so dramatically, so can Christian. But I'm worried about you. I have the feeling you're headed for a terrible disaster, as usual, and I don't want to see you hurt."

Jessica's feelings softened toward her sister. "Don't worry, Liz. Christian has promised me he won't participate in any violence whatsoever and I believe him."

"I know you do," Elizabeth said. "But when Ken tells the rest of the SVH guys what happened . . ." She swallowed, and looked at her sister with tear-stained eyes. "Christian may not have any choice."

Chapter 3

"Come on, Liz," Enid said, tapping her foot impatiently. "We're going to be late for homeroom."

Elizabeth stood in front of her open locker on Monday morning, her gaze searching the neatly organized contents for . . . *something*. "Oh, great," she muttered. "Now I can't even remember what it is I'm looking for."

"Are you okay?" Enid asked.

Elizabeth glanced at Enid, noting her look of concern. "I'm fine," she said with a deep sigh.

"Sure you are. And those dark circles under your eyes are a new makeup trick to enhance your good looks."

"Very funny," Elizabeth said. "Oh yeah, now I remember what it was—my math notebook. I can't find it anywhere."

Enid looked at the books in Elizabeth's arms. "Isn't that it?" she asked, tapping the green spiral-bound notebook on top of the pile.

Elizabeth blinked with disbelief. "Okay, so maybe you're right. I'm not fine. To tell you the truth, I'm tired, cranky, and I'm having a terrible morning." She shut her locker and turned to Enid. "I can't seem to focus on anything."

"You look exhausted," Enid said.

Elizabeth shrugged. "I am. I don't think I slept more than an hour or two last night. Every time I'd shut my eyes, my mind would start spinning nightmares—the kind which seem to be coming true."

"Todd hasn't called you?" Enid asked.

Elizabeth shook her head sadly. She hadn't called him, either.

Her relationship with Todd had become shaky over the past few weeks because of their disagreement over the school rivalry. But shortly before the trouble had started on Saturday night, Elizabeth and Todd had begun to patch things up. They'd vowed not to let anything come between them again.

Now Elizabeth wasn't so sure their vow would hold up. It hurt her to think that their relationship might become a casualty of war. But she'd seen it happen to Caitlin Alexander, her friend from Palisades. Caitlin and her long-time boyfriend, Doug Riker, had recently split up. Now Doug was seeing another girl and Caitlin was nursing a broken heart.

"You must have been worried sick about Todd," Enid said.

And Jessica, Elizabeth mentally added. But she wasn't ready to talk about her sister and Christian Gorman. Enid wouldn't understand what was going on with Jessica. Elizabeth barely understood it herself.

"Well, I have some good news for you," Enid said. "Maria told me that Bruce's father and Todd's parents went down to the station Saturday night and posted bond for them."

"That's a relief. I hated the thought of Todd and Bruce having to spend the whole night in a jail cell." Elizabeth shut her locker and took a deep breath. "I suppose I should go talk to Todd," she said, a hint of reluctance in her voice.

"Don't worry," Enid said. "I'm sure he's not still angry with you for calling the police."

"I don't know what to expect from him," Elizabeth said. "I keep seeing that angry look on his face."

"Let's go," Enid said, tugging on Elizabeth's arm. "You and Todd have been together for too long to let something like this come between you."

Enid was right. No matter what had happened between them, Elizabeth wasn't ready to give up on her relationship with Todd—not without a struggle. She was ready to put the anger and violence behind them and hopefully, so was he.

Todd was standing by his locker, talking with Bruce, Tad "Blubber" Johnson, Aaron Dallas, Ricky Ordway, and a few other guys. When Elizabeth and Enid walked over to them, the conversation suddenly stopped. Todd glanced at Elizabeth. His coffee brown eyes, usually so warm and open, were hard and cold.

Elizabeth drew in a long breath. "Hello, Todd," she said softly. "I'm glad everything turned out okay."

He turned his back to her and shut his locker. "I'll see you later, Bruce."

"Todd?" she said, taking a step toward him. He walked right by her as though she were invisible.

Her heart sank. "Todd, please!" she called after him. "Talk to me."

He kept right on walking, completely ignoring her. She blinked back the tears stinging her eyes.

Bruce slammed his locker shut and turned to her. "What did you expect, Wakefield?"

Caroline Pearce, always on the alert for juicy gossip, was watching the exchange, her green eyes flashing with interest. "What's wrong with Todd?" she asked, patting her red hair into place, as if the gesture might lend an element of casualness to her curiosity.

Ricky Ordway, whose arm was wrapped in a massive bandage, turned to Elizabeth with a snide look. "Gee, I don't know," he said sarcastically. "Maybe Todd is upset about the knife his girlfriend stuck in his back?"

"That's not fair," Enid said, coming to Elizabeth's defense.

Olivia Davidson, whose locker was nearby, also spoke up. "I don't know all the details of what happened Saturday night, but I do know Elizabeth would never betray a friend. Especially not Todd." Olivia was the arts editor for *The Oracle* and a close friend of Elizabeth's.

"Well, I *was* there," Maria said, walking over to stand beside Elizabeth. "And I say you guys are acting like idiots. If Elizabeth hadn't called the police, who knows what might have happened."

"We would have gotten revenge," Ricky said, lifting his bandaged arm.

"With all that vicious fighting," Maria countered, "it's a wonder one of you wasn't killed or maimed. I'd say you're lucky they could put you back together with only a few stitches."

"Oh sure," Bruce sneered. "If it were up to Elizabeth, Todd could rot in jail forever."

The accusation cut deeply. "That's not true," Elizabeth said, her voice trembling.

"Oh yeah?" Bruce shouted, his icy blue eyes

40

filled with anger. "Why then didn't you come to the jail Saturday night? Todd was a mess. It would've meant a lot to him to know you were there for him, that you cared."

"I just . . . couldn't," she stammered.

"You couldn't be bothered, you mean. Even Winston, with a bandaged nose and a black eye, managed to stop by to offer moral support. Why couldn't you?" He pointed his finger close to her face. "I'll tell you why," he growled, answering his own question. "Because when it comes right down to it, a guy can only depend on his buddies. A girlfriend will stand by you if everything is going okay, but when your back is against the wall, she'll ditch you as fast as she can."

A few of the guys murmured in agreement, while several of the girls gasped in outrage.

"When loyalty counts," Bruce continued, "it's the guys you can trust."

Maria stepped forward. "Trust them to act like Neanderthals, you mean."

The girls nodded, several chiming in with similar statements.

"Can't you guys see how ridiculous this whole rivalry is?" Enid said, shaking her head.

Like the signal for the end of a round of a boxing match, the bell rang. The group dispersed as everyone rushed to their classrooms. Elizabeth walked away with a heavy feeling in her chest. She wished she could forget about the Sweet Valley-Palisades War for even a few minutes, but she soon realized that was impossible. The entire school was talking about it. All morning long, in her classes, in the girls' room, in the corridors—everywhere Elizabeth went, she overheard snatches of the same argument:

"We're going to get those Palisades creeps!" Ron Edwards proclaimed.

"And then they're going to get you right back, so big deal," Olivia Davidson replied as she passed Ron in the hall.

"We'll teach those Palisades scumbags a lesson they'll never forget," Tim Nelson bragged.

Dana Larson turned to him with a wry expression. "Oh great," she said, "idiots teaching idiots."

It was painfully obvious to Elizabeth that Sweet Valley High had divided into two camps; the guys wanted to make war with Palisades High and the girls wanted to end the violence. There *had* to be a way to make the guys listen to reason.

By midmorning, Jessica had come to the conclusion that guilt was absolutely the worst emotion. She normally wasn't the type to dwell on her mistakes and usually managed to avoid feeling guilty quite well. But today it wrapped itself around her neck like thick iron chains, pulling her to the ground, choking her.

She knew she wouldn't have any peace of mind

until she faced up to what she'd done to Ken. At the very least, he deserved an apology.

During third period, which she knew Ken had free, Jessica cut her class in order to speak with him. She stopped in the girls' room to fix her makeup and was dismayed to see how pale and lifeless her complexion was. The yellow silk tank top she wore, which she'd borrowed from Lila ages ago, made her look completely washed out and frumpy.

She reapplied a layer of burnt rose lipstick, swept her cheeks with ginger-flower blush, and brushed her hair. She even tried smiling at her reflection. The haggard shadows remained.

Come on, girl! she mentally scolded herself. *You're just stalling for time.*

Jessica found Ken outside on the football field, tossing a ball with a few of the guys. He didn't see her at first. She stood quietly on the sideline, gathering her courage. The field had been mowed recently and the sweet fragrance of freshly cut grass lingered in the air.

Ken really is a natural athlete, she thought, watching him admiringly. His movements were strong and graceful. The dark blue T-shirt he wore highlighted his tanned muscular arms and his wind-tossed, sandy blond hair. Shading her eyes, she watched as he raised the football over his head and with flawless precision, shot a pass across the field to Danny Porter.

Suddenly he turned and saw her. His expression hardened, without a hint of welcome. He didn't make a move toward her, standing still as though the sight of her had turned him to stone. For one heart-stopping moment, Jessica was afraid he would turn around and walk away without giving her a chance to speak.

Finally, he waved to the guys and jogged over to her. "What do you want, Jessica?" he asked, his gaze shifting across her forehead, behind her, to the side . . . everywhere but directly into her eyes.

She couldn't help remembering how much they'd meant to each other just a short time ago. "Ken, I want to explain how sorry I am," she said.

He scowled at her, his face etched with pain. "Sorry? The great Jessica Wakefield is *sorry*? You're kidding, right?"

"Of course I'm not kidding," Jessica protested. "Hurting you like I did—" She exhaled a long, shaky breath. Hundreds of sweet memories of her and Ken flashed through her mind. She remembered the thrill of their first kiss at the victory barbecue after the SVH-Big Mesa football game. Ken had thrown the winning pass and Jessica had felt so proud and happy. She could recall how romantic it was, sitting with him on her beach blanket. Her stomach had fluttered out of control and when their lips had touched . . .

Then there was the time when she and the cheerleading squad had gone to Yosemite for the national cheerleading competition. Boys weren't allowed to visit, but that hadn't stopped Ken and some of the other guys from sneaking into the compound. They'd dressed up as female cheerleaders—the tallest and *ugliest* anyone had ever seen—and masqueraded as the squad from Saskatchewan. It had touched her that Ken had gone to so much trouble to see her, but it was the funniest thing she'd ever seen.

Ken had been her shining hero and her dear friend. They had shared so many great times. How could he possibly doubt her feelings of remorse? *My heart feels like it's dying,* she thought. "I can't begin to tell you how sorry I am," she said. "I know this was all my fault." Her voice trembled.

"Wow! You're really sorry," he said. "I guess there's a first time for everything. Have you told Elizabeth yet? I'm sure she'll want to write an article about it for *The Oracle*."

"Oh, Ken, you have to believe me," she pleaded. A strong breeze whipped a lock of her hair across her face. She pushed it back, absently noticing that her cheeks were damp with tears. "I never planned to fall in love with Christian. It just happened."

He shook his head, staring at her with a look of rancor. "Things like that don't just 'happen.' You'll have to come up with a better line."

45

"But it did, really," she said.

"Oh, sure. And your mouth just happened to become fused with his as you were walking into the restaurant." He paused, running his teeth over his bottom lip, his gaze never leaving her face. "Tell me something, Jessica," he said, "does that sort of thing *just happen* to you often?"

"I know it looked awful, but I never meant to hurt you."

"Yeah, it did look bad. But don't worry about me. The biggest mistake I ever made was believing anything you said. And I'll never do that again," he added.

Jessica sniffed. "I wish there was something I could do to make it up to you."

"There is," Ken replied. "Stay away from me."

Jessica closed her eyes. A cascade of hot tears escaped, soaking her cheeks. "I don't blame you if you hate me." She opened her eyes and looked at him through a watery veil. "I know what I did was terrible."

Ken took a deep breath and looked into her eyes. "No, I don't hate you, Jessica. I only wish, if you had to cheat on me, it would have been with someone better than Christian Gorman."

Jessica resisted the urge to defend Christian and the love they shared. Ken was too hurt to listen, let alone understand. After all they'd been through together, she realized with regret that it would be impossible for them to have a rational conversation.

"I guess it's over between us," Ken said.

Jessica nodded. She opened her mouth to speak, but Ken cut her off.

"I know, I know. You're sorry," he said.

She nodded again, hot tears streaming down her face. Ken's eyes softened for an instant as he reached out and tucked an errant strand of her hair behind her ear. The gentleness of the gesture crushed Jessica's heart more than his anger ever could.

"For what it's worth," he said, his eyes filling with tears, "I'm sorry, too."

Elizabeth stared at the open carton of lemon yogurt on her tray without seeing it. The noisy clatter of the lunch room sounded far away, like traffic buzzing along a distant highway. Her mind struggled to make sense of the chaos which seemed to have engulfed her world. The ever-efficient Sweet Valley High gossip grapevine had outdone itself this time, spreading tales about the Wakefield twins throughout the school with lightning speed. Every student had learned two facts that morning, no matter what classes they attended: Elizabeth called the police on Saturday night and Jessica cheated on Ken Matthews with Christian Gorman.

Elizabeth looked up to see Jessica approaching her table. Although they rarely ever sat together at lunch, she wasn't surprised when Jessica took the seat next to her. It didn't matter how different they were; when times got tough, the Wakefield twins stuck together.

Jessica peeled the cellophane wrapper from a package of chocolate chip cookies, but didn't make a move to eat them. Lila and Amy carried their lunch trays over and sat down. Enid, Olivia, and a few other girls followed.

One of the reasons why she and Jessica usually sat at different tables was that they each had a circle of friends which didn't mix well with the other's. Elizabeth found Jessica's cheerleader bunch, with their constant chatter about boys, clothes, and new cheer routines, utterly boring, while Jessica often complained that Elizabeth's friends seemed lifeless and morbidly serious. And their best friends, Lila and Enid, rarely even acknowledged each other's existence. But because Elizabeth and Jessica were sitting together, a mismatched group of girls gathered at their lunch table.

It seemed perfectly appropriate to Elizabeth. *After all, strangers often turn to one another in times of crisis*, she thought.

The mood at the table was somber and quiet. Elizabeth and Jessica looked at each other, communicating their shared feelings of misery with their eyes.

Finally Maria spoke. "Elizabeth and Jessica, I hate to tell you this, but I think you two ought to know.

Winston told me that someone wrote your phone number on the wall in the boys' room, with the message, 'For a good back-stab, call the Wakefield babes.'"

Enid's eyes flashed with a look of indignation. "Those creeps!"

"Who do you think actually wrote it?" Caroline asked with open curiosity.

"It doesn't matter," Elizabeth said. "I just wish they'd all grow up and get over this nonsense before someone really gets hurt."

"They're really steamed up about Jessica and Christian Gorman," Sandy Bacon said. Sandy was a cheerleader and a friend of Jessica's.

Amy Sutton took a sip from her milk carton and set it down on her tray. "I think the guys might eventually be able to forgive Elizabeth for calling the police. But I don't know about you, Jessica. Kissing up to the enemy is serious. I think they actually execute people who do that during a war."

"Isn't that an uplifting bit of information," Enid said, glaring across the table at Amy. "Thanks for sharing it."

Amy stared back in wide-eyed innocence. "It's true."

"Yes, we know," Olivia said, a note of irritation in her voice.

"There has to be a way to put an end to this craziness," Elizabeth said.

"Don't look now," Lila said, ducking her head. "Here comes the goon squad."

Elizabeth looked up to see Bruce Patman, Aaron Dallas, Kirk Anderson, and Danny Porter sit at the table next to hers. Winston joined them a moment later, with a slight smile and a look of apology in Maria's direction. His nose was covered with a thick white bandage with two air holes for him to breathe and the area around his left eye was brownish blue and swollen. Looking at him, Elizabeth felt the impact of this horrible rivalry. *Why can't the guys understand?* she wondered.

Suddenly, Bruce lifted his head and sniffed at the air. "Do you guys smell something bad?" he asked in a loud voice. Several students from nearby tables turned to look.

"Yeah, now that you mention it," Kirk answered. He brushed back his jet black hair and smiled arrogantly. "Smells like something rotten."

"It must be the 'Palisades stink' coming from Jessica Wakefield's table," Aaron said. "I hear it gets on a person and you just can't wash it off."

Danny laughed. "Yeah, it's worse than being sprayed by a skunk. Even taking a bath in tomato juice won't work."

"Hey, Jessica," Kirk said, "is your new boyfriend going to let you wear his flea collar when you two go steady?"

The guys broke up with peals of laughter. Even Winston was chuckling. "Good one, Kirk," Aaron said, slapping his knee.

Jessica was on the verge of tears, which pushed Elizabeth to her limit. She stood up and turned to the guys, anger rushing through her like molten lava. "Who do you think you are, telling Jessica who she can and can't go out with! You guys make me sick. You have no right to judge her or anyone else.

"Try looking at yourselves instead," Elizabeth continued. "You all act so big and tough, but I've never seen a more ridiculous bunch of idiots in my life. Where is all this headed? Are you guys planning to march into Palisades High School and occupy their building? But why stop there? Why not keep going—conquer the elementary school too, while you're at it. That would really make you feel like heroes, wouldn't it?"

She paused, studying their faces. "I think you guys have been watching too many violent cartoons. Why don't you shut off the TV and grow up!"

"Way to go, Liz," Olivia softly cheered.

Bruce glared at Elizabeth, his cheeks flushed with red anger. "Are you through?"

She refused to be intimidated. "No, I'm not," she answered, meeting his rage with her own. "I have one more thing to say. Until this rivalry with Palisades High is over, none of the Sweet Valley girls

51

will have anything to do with you or any of the guys. Your girlfriends won't go out with you, or kiss you, or help you with your homework, or listen sympathetically to all your problems—everything stops until you guys start acting like civilized human beings."

A hush fell over the area. Realizing what she'd just said, Elizabeth gulped, wishing she could take back her words. She'd spoken without thinking, caught up in the heat of the argument. She stood there trembling, terrified that none of the girls would back her up on the no-boyfriends ultimatum. She should've discussed the plan with them first, instead of blurting it out impulsively.

The guys answered with jeering laughter. "*Our* girlfriends would never do that to us," Danny said. "We're a lot luckier than Todd and Ken."

"Yeah," Kirk said. "Some guys have girlfriends who are actually loyal. That's a concept you and your sister wouldn't understand."

No one at the girls' table uttered a sound. Elizabeth stood perfectly still, her heart slamming wildly against her rib cage. Finally, Maria broke the tense silence. She glanced over at Winston and shrugged. "Sorry," she said. "World peace is more important."

"Than me?" Winston asked

"No. But it is more important than hanging out with you at the Dairi Burger or driving up to Miller's Point."

"I can't believe you're doing this, Maria!" Winston protested. Bruce patted him on the shoulder in a display of empathy.

Then Pamela Robertson spoke up. "I'm with you too, Elizabeth." Pamela and Bruce had been dating on and off for some time and had recently gotten back together.

Bruce glared at her with a threatening glint in his eyes. "You'd better think long and hard about this, Pamela."

She stood up, facing him with a look of pure, feminine power. "And you'd better think about what it's costing you to act like a caveman."

Claire Middleton, who was sitting at the table directly behind Elizabeth, got up and turned to Danny, her boyfriend. Normally shy, Claire's voice rang out strong and clear. "Me, too. I'm sick and tired of all this fighting. I want it to stop and I'll do whatever it takes."

"Oh man," Danny groaned, wiping his hand over his face.

"I'm warning you, Pamela," Bruce was saying.

Pamela ignored him. The girls turned their backs on the guys and exchanged looks of triumph. "So, did any of you catch the new movie playing at the Valley Cinema?" Olivia said, her voice deceptively casual.

"I did and it was marvelous," Lila gushed with a

twinkle of amusement. "I just adore Brad Pitt, don't you? All that rugged charm . . ."

"Oh, yeah," Amy said. "Brad Pitt is so much better looking than those old geezers Elizabeth and Enid like."

"Humphrey Bogart is not an old geezer," Enid protested. She turned to Elizabeth and smiled. "Can you imagine anyone saying that about the greatest actor who ever lived?"

"No, I can't," Elizabeth softly replied. A warm feeling came over her as she looked around the table. She was relieved that the girls had gone along with her, but she was even more proud of them for standing up to the guys. The Sweet Valley High girls proved they were made of strong stuff and she was honored to be one of them. "Humphrey Bogart could eat Brad Pitt for lunch," she said with a smile.

Disgusted, Bruce threw his uneaten sandwich down on his lunch tray. Those girls made him sick. Jessica and Elizabeth—even Pamela—could jump off the nearest pier and drown themselves as far as he was concerned. They were sitting there so smugly, chatting mindlessly about movie actors as if nothing were wrong. He knew they were doing it just to make him and the guys mad. And it was working. He was furious.

Didn't they realize how important it was for Sweet Valley High to stand up to those jerks from Palisades? It wasn't fair. The guys were taking all the risks and the girls didn't even have the decency to support them.

He couldn't decide whether it was loyalty they lacked or the brains to see what Palisades High was doing to their school. Maybe it was a combination of both—the Sweet Valley High girls were traitors *and* hopelessly dumb.

The other guys were watching him, waiting for his next move. But Bruce was too angry to think straight. What he wanted desperately to do was throw his orange plastic lunch tray at Elizabeth Wakefield's head, and then his chair at Jessica's. He looked down and noticed his hands were curled into fists.

"Why don't we move to a different table," Winston suggested.

"Good idea," Kirk said. "Let's find a table that isn't downwind of the skunk club."

The guys stood up, their chairs scraping the floor in unison. Before stomping off with the others, Bruce turned to Jessica, a fierce look gleaming in his eyes. "You're going to pay, Wakefield," he said. "And I mean big."

Chapter 4

Jessica closed her eyes, reeling from Bruce's cutting remarks. When she opened them again, everyone around her appeared to be moving in slow motion. The cafeteria walls seemed to be shifting, closing in on her. She felt as if she were sinking right through her chair and down into the ground.

She took a deep breath, trying to clear her mind. Her stomach growled, reminding her she hadn't eaten anything at all since yesterday afternoon. But everything on her tray looked disgusting.

All around the table, Elizabeth and the other girls were talking rapidly. Jessica couldn't figure out what they were saying, their conversation spinning and squeaking like a cassette tape wound too tightly. The room turned into a blur of color. A wave of nausea crashed over her, immediately followed by a wave of dizziness. She couldn't catch her breath. She felt as if she were caught in a rip tide and drowning fast.

Leaving her lunch tray on the table, Jessica jumped up and ran to the exit. Outside, she sank down on a bench and struggled for air, gasping for each breath.

"What's the matter?" Elizabeth asked.

Jessica looked up to see her sister standing over her with a look of concern. She tried to speak, but could only manage an inarticulate grunt.

Elizabeth sat down beside her. "Are you sick?" she asked.

Jessica drew in a long breath and shook her head. "I'll be all right. I just had to get out of there. You didn't have to follow me."

"I was worried."

"I know." Jessica reached out and squeezed Elizabeth's hand. "But I just needed to be alone."

"Well," Elizabeth said, rising from the bench. "If you're sure you're okay."

Jessica nodded. "Oh, and by the way," she said as Elizabeth turned to leave, "thanks. For sticking up for me."

"That's what big sisters are for," Elizabeth replied. With a final wave, she went back inside the building.

Alone, Jessica indulged her feelings of sadness,

letting the tears flow freely down her face. "Oh, Christian," she whispered. A feeling of desolation came over her. All around her, the elements of a gorgeous day seem to mock her—the brightly shining sun, the clear blue sky, the colorful blossoms decorating the school grounds—making her feel even worse.

Draping her arm along the back of the bench, she lowered her head and rested her forehead against the crook of her elbow. She loved Christian so much, her heart ached. She'd given up trying to make anyone understand how deeply they cared for each other. All she wanted now was for people just to leave them alone.

If only he were with me now, she thought wistfully. His arms wrapped around her would chase away all of her gloom, she was certain. She tried to imagine where he was at that moment, what he was doing.

The sound of screeching tires grabbed her attention. She looked up to see a blue Volkswagen bus swerving into the school lot. Jessica blinked in disbelief. She wondered if her dreams of Christian had turned into hallucinations.

But no—it really was him! She ran to the van, her heart leaping with joy. As soon as she jumped in, Christian pulled her into his arms. Jessica wrapped her arms around his neck and sighed deeply. A wonderful feeling of coming home flowed through her entire body.

She leaned back, looking into his smoky blue eyes with awe. "How did you know I needed you right now?" she asked.

He kissed her. "Because I needed you."

"No, I mean it," she insisted. "I was just sitting over there thinking about you, wondering what you were doing and missing you terribly."

"And here I am, surfer girl."

"Oh, Christian," she said, "you really are my knight in shining armor."

He smiled tenderly. "And you're the sweetest princess I know."

Jessica reached for the passenger-side seat belt and pulled it across her chest. "Come on, let's see how fast you can rescue me from this monstrous prison," she said. "I've had about as much of Sweet Valley High as I can stand for today."

"Are you in a hurry to get home?" Todd asked as he maneuvered his Mercedes out of the school parking lot. His gaze shifted from the windshield to Ken, who was slumped down in the passenger seat, staring out the window.

"No," Ken answered, his expression flat.

Todd didn't try to start a conversation. It had been a long, harrowing day for both of them. He knew Ken's world was spinning out of control as fast as his own. All day long Todd had been unable to concentrate on anything. His brain felt as if it were packed on ice like a medical specimen.

He turned onto a narrow dirt road and followed the same path he'd taken Saturday night. He wasn't sure why he needed to return. He only knew he had to.

When they arrived at the abandoned warehouse, Todd hesitated, letting the engine idle as he stared at the brick building. He was suddenly afraid of what he might discover. Ken turned to him, frowning. "What are we doing here?"

Todd shrugged. "I don't know. I guess I just wanted to see what the place looks like in daylight." He pushed open the door and jumped out of the car. As he walked across the gravel parking lot, Ken caught up with him.

"This place is a mess," Ken said.

Todd nodded solemnly. The area around the warehouse showed the scars of Saturday's battle. The tall grass and weeds growing here and there on the lot were bent over, crushed by the cars which had driven over them in such heated urgency. Where the ground was bare, the soft dirt was crisscrossed with tire tracks. The building itself looked like an injured old man who'd had the stuffing beaten out of him. Every window was broken, all of them reduced to gaping holes, jagged slivers of glass, and spider cracks.

The side door was hanging on its hinges. Todd vaguely remembered that it had been locked and they'd crashed through it with brute force. Ken pushed it open and walked in. With a feeling of trepidation, Todd followed.

Inside, the damage was unbelievable. Even with the small amount of sunlight filtering through the high, narrow windows, Todd could see the place had been ravaged. He looked around, shocked. Broken glass was scattered everywhere, crunching under his feet as he walked across the cement floor. Splintered pieces of wooden pallets were strewn about; the guys had ripped off the deckboards for makeshift weapons and, brandishing their wooden swords, had charged the enemy like medieval crusaders.

But, Todd reminded himself, *I've never read a history book or watched a PBS documentary that said that the Crusades were a good idea.* He kicked at a clump of leather and saw it was a piece of someone's belt. Under one of the windows, the wall was smeared with a brown streak. Todd looked closer and recoiled in horror when he discovered it was blood. Ken was standing behind him, his expression also grim.

"This place looks like it's been through a bomb raid," Ken said, shaking his head.

"I can't believe we're right in the middle of all

this," Todd said. "Even when I got arrested, the whole thing didn't seem real."

Ken buried his hands in the pocket of his denim jacket. "What do you mean?" he asked.

"There we were," Todd began, remembering, "Bruce and I, in a cell with Greg McMullen and this other guy from Palisades. At first I thought we could work something out, come up with some kind of a compromise between the four of us. The next thing I knew, I was slamming my fist into McMullen's face. It was as if the real me had gone away and a machine took over my body. I didn't feel a thing."

"Then what happened?" Ken asked.

Todd wiped his hand over his face and cupped his chin. "They dragged me off of him and threw me into a different cell by myself. Then it hit me— my real self came back and I realized I was in deep trouble. I wanted to scream and yell, tell them they'd made a big mistake, that they'd arrested the wrong guy. It was something out of a nightmare." He tossed a broken stick across the floor. "I guess that's why I wanted to come here today—to see if Saturday night really happened."

Ken sat down on a pallet and braced his elbows on his knees. "I can't believe Jessica ditched me for one of their goons. *Christian Gorman!* She cheated on me with that idiot loser." He turned to Todd. "You know, she was acting pretty weird all week. I thought it was because I wasn't paying enough attention to her. What a stupid jerk I am! All the time she was sneaking behind my back and sucking face with a Palisades slug. Some girlfriend Jessica Wakefield turned out to be, huh?"

"Tell me about it," Todd said bitterly. "*My* girlfriend isn't exactly Ms. Loyalty, either. I spent most of Saturday night in jail because Elizabeth had me arrested. Who knows what will happen at my court hearing tomorrow?"

As they walked to the exit, Ken paused for one last look around the devastated site. "I wonder how everything fell apart so quickly," he said.

"Say that again," Jessica demanded, hugging Christian's arm as they walked hand in hand down the beach, cool sea foam lapping over their feet. She felt as though she'd stepped into a glorious dream. The day, which had started with such a miserable morning, turned out to be perfect. A soft breeze fluttered through her hair. She and Christian were surrounded by the sounds of calling seagulls and crashing waves, and by the rich fragrance of salty air.

After Christian had picked her up at school during lunch, they'd driven to the small strip of beach north of Moon Beach where they usually met in the morning for her surfing lessons. It was their own special place and, in Jessica's opinion, the most beautiful spot on earth.

There they'd spent the entire afternoon surfing. It didn't matter to Jessica that she'd missed her sixth-period chemistry exam. She'd lost track of how many classes she'd skipped during the last couple weeks. Nor did it matter that the consequence for leaving the school building before the end of the day without permission was suspension. Academics and school rules had never been very important to her. Now that she was falling in love and living through a war, they meant even less.

Christian smiled at her, a glint of amusement in his gorgeous, smoky blue eyes. "Say what again? That I'm hungry and want a pizza?" he teased.

"No," she replied, tickling his waist. "You know what I mean. Tell me again what a great surfer I am and how I have a shot at winning the competition."

"Are you sure that's what I said? Funny, but I can't seem to remember," he said.

"Oh no? Well, let me help you." Jessica was wearing a loose, cotton shirt of Christian's over her red string bikini. Following a devilish impulse, she took the shirt off and dipped it in the water. "This will refresh your memory," she said with a laugh as she flung the cold, soaking shirt across Christian's sun-warmed back. "It'll refresh you, anyway."

He gasped, his whole body clenched for an instant. Then he turned slowly, stalking her like a cat after prey. "That wasn't very nice of you, surfer girl."

She giggled nervously, her stomach fluttering with anticipation as she slowly backed away from him. He moved closer and just as she figured out she ought to start running, he grabbed her.

Christian hauled her up in his arms and carried her kicking and screaming into the water, where he dropped her with a huge splash. Jessica came up sputtering, hungry for retaliation. As he stood there laughing at her, she pushed her hand across of the surface of the water, splashing him right in the mouth. Then she started running as fast as she could.

Thrashing about in the surf with Christian close behind, Jessica couldn't remember having more fun in her entire life.

"Why do I feel as if I should be wearing a disguise?" Elizabeth asked as she turned her Jeep into the front drive of Palisades High. She, Enid, and Olivia had come to meet with Marla and Caitlin to discuss the latest developments in their schools' rivalry. After the heated confrontation with the SVH guys at lunch, the girls had decided that their no-dates strategy would be more effective if it came from both sides of the war.

"Because we're on enemy territory," Enid answered, studying the pale concrete building. "I don't see any cannons pointed at us, though. So maybe we'll survive."

"I don't know," Olivia said, tossing back her mane of curly brown hair. "The last time we were here, Elizabeth and I ran into some dangerous-looking characters."

"Don't remind me," Elizabeth groaned. She and Olivia had visited Palisades High a few weeks before to gather material for a special edition of *The Oracle*. The PH students had reacted with suspicion and hostility, as if she and Olivia were enemy spies. Marla and Caitlin had been treated the same way at SVH.

Elizabeth parked in a far corner of the parking lot, behind a green Dumpster, hoping her black Jeep wouldn't draw too much attention.

"You're sure Marla and Caitlin know we're coming?" Enid asked.

Elizabeth nodded. She had contacted them by E-mail, from the computer in the *Oracle* office to the one at the *Palisades Pentagon*. "There was a message from Marla when I checked the computer during seventh period. She said they would be waiting for us by the door on the west side of the building."

"Okay, then," Olivia said, pushing open the passenger door. "Let's get on with our mission."

Elizabeth drew in a deep breath. "And let's hope this works better than our other attempts. I don't

66

know if I can take any more full-scale disasters."

"Come on, don't be such a pessimist," Enid said. "Oh look, there they are." Enid waved to Marla and Caitlin, who were walking across the parking lot toward them.

"We were watching for you," Caitlin said. She was taller than Elizabeth, with short, choppy black hair. Although her smile was friendly and welcoming, Elizabeth saw a trace of sadness in her almond-shaped brown eyes. Breaking up with Doug had hurt her deeply.

"I was so happy when I got your message, Elizabeth," Marla said. "We've been trying to figure out what's going on." A gust of wind blew her curly red hair across her face. Without missing a beat in the conversation, Marla pulled a blue bandanna out of her jeans pocket and, grabbing the wild mass with one hand, deftly wrapped it up into a fabric-covered chignon. "Some of the PH guys were arrested Saturday. Did you know?"

Elizabeth, Enid, and Olivia exchanged meaningful looks. "Yes, we did," Elizabeth said. "So was Bruce Patman—and Todd."

Caitlin and Marla gasped. "I'm sorry," Caitlin said. "Oh, Elizabeth, you must be devastated."

Elizabeth shrugged. "So what else is new?"

"Let's go sit down," Marla said, pointing to the aluminum bleachers on the field next to the parking lot. "Seems we have a lot of catching up to do."

"The rumors around here are flying like crazy," Caitlin said. "I don't know what's true and what's being made up for the sake of propaganda. We're hearing that the SVH guys attacked the PH guys at an abandoned warehouse on Saturday night for no reason at all."

Enid stopped in her tracks. "What! *For no reason at all?* I don't think so. The Palisades guys kidnapped Winston Egbert and beat him senseless. He has a broken nose and a black eye."

The girls resumed walking. "Seems that part of the story was conveniently left out," Caitlin said.

Marla's green eyes sparkled with anger. "I think I hate that most of all," she said. "The distorted press coverage this war is getting."

Olivia chuckled. "Spoken like a true newspaper editor-in-chief."

They reached the bleachers and climbed halfway up to the top where they could be sure of complete privacy. "Spies and gossipmongers are everywhere," Marla said in a spooky sounding voice.

"It makes sense," Caitlin began.

"What does?" Elizabeth asked.

"The PH guys kidnapped Winston to get back at him for slashing the tires on Jack Watson's Corolla last Tuesday. Now it's the SVH guys' turn to do something outrageous. They're completely out of control."

Elizabeth sighed. "It's all so strange. Winston is a

happy, easygoing, class-clown sort of guy. And Todd is usually so sweet and thoughtful. It's as if they've undergone complete personality transplants."

A few tears fell from Caitlin's eyes. She wiped them with the back of her hand and sniffed. "Don't mind me," she said, flashing a tremulous smile.

"Maybe you and Doug will get back together after this is all over," Enid said.

Marla rolled her eyes upward. "I hope not."

"What do you mean?" Elizabeth asked.

Marla turned to Caitlin with a pointed look. "What she means," Caitlin said, "is that I walked in on Doug and Britta Jantzen going at it in the science hall this morning. They were all over each other."

"Maybe he's just putting on a show to make you jealous," Enid suggested.

Caitlin snorted. "Yeah, well it did more than that. It made me sick. If that's the sort of trick he's going to pull when we have a disagreement, I'm better off without him."

Elizabeth nodded sadly, wondering if she and Todd would suffer the same fate.

"You're better off without him," Marla insisted. "But, getting back to the madness at hand, what more can we do? After everything we've tried already, I feel like the situation's hopeless."

Enid sat up straight. "I'm glad you asked that question. Elizabeth has come up with a dynamite plan that just might convince the guys to call a truce."

All eyes turned to Elizabeth. She held up her hands. "I don't know if I'd call it 'dynamite' exactly. The Sweet Valley High girls have issued the guys an ultimatum: Until the war is over, their girlfriends will have nothing whatsoever to do with them."

"We call it the no-dates plan," Enid added.

Caitlin and Marla looked at each other. "It could work," Caitlin said.

Marla nodded. "I like it. It's simple and to the point. Are most of the SVH girls going along with it?"

Elizabeth beamed with pride. "Yes. We decided all this during lunch this afternoon and by the end of the day, our pact was cinched solid."

"That's great," Marla said.

"It would be better if the Palisades High girls did the same thing," Olivia said. "Then both sides would be under pressure to make peace."

"The girls here are just as sick of the fighting as we are," Caitlin said. "I'm sure they'll be willing to quit their boyfriends for such a noble cause. Except for Britta Jantzen, of course. She's a complete moron. I'm sure that's what Doug likes about her."

Marla glanced over Elizabeth's shoulder. "Uh oh," she muttered. "Here comes Rosie Shaw."

Elizabeth turned and saw a tough looking girl with short reddish brown hair approaching the bleachers. She wore a black leather jacket and faded blue jeans which were ripped across each thigh. She had the lean, muscular build of an athlete and walked with a steady, confident stride.

It took Elizabeth only a moment to remember where she'd heard that name. "My sister, Jessica, mentioned her. She's a competitive surfer, isn't she?"

"She's also Greg McMullen's girlfriend," Caitlin said.

"Do you think she'll join our no-dates plan?" Olivia asked.

Marla snorted. "Don't count on it. Rosie is so much more than just Greg's girlfriend. She's sort of like . . . his trained Doberman pinscher."

"Pit bull is more like it," Caitlin grumbled.

Elizabeth watched as Rosie Shaw climbed up toward them, moving with sure-footed agility and grace. She was wearing dark sunglasses which hid her eyes. Elizabeth realized that she'd seen her before—and stayed away. When Elizabeth and Olivia had visited Palisades High the week before, Elizabeth had made a special point of not trying to interview her. There was something about her that shot off a warning in Elizabeth's head. Rosie Shaw seemed to carry bad vibes around with her.

Elizabeth braced herself for a confrontation, but to her surprise, Rosie approached them with a warm, friendly smile. Caitlin and Marla were watching her warily.

71

Rosie sat down on the next bleacher, facing them. "Hi, everyone," she said. "What's up?"

Marla shrugged her shoulder. "Not much."

"The latest issue of the *Palisades Pentagon* looks great. I loved the story about the proposed renovations for the library and west wing. It makes me feel so good to know you guys are keeping tabs on the Board of Ed."

"Thanks," Caitlin answered flatly.

Rosie continued. "I really have a lot of respect for all the work you're doing. It can't be easy to produce such a high-quality school paper." She turned to Elizabeth, Enid, and Olivia. "By the way, I'm Rosie Shaw."

The SVH girls introduced themselves. "I'm so pleased to meet you guys," Rosie said. "Just so you know, I've also read *The Oracle.* The article you guys did on the history of Palisades High was fabulous." She turned to Olivia. "And the photos were great. You're a very talented photographer," she said.

"Thanks," Olivia muttered.

Rosie looked at Caitlin and Marla, who were still staring at her with open suspicion, and giggled. "Okay, I'll admit it. I have an ulterior motive for coming over here."

"Oh, *really?* I never would have guessed," Marla said.

Rosie smiled sweetly and turned to Elizabeth. "Actually, I wanted to meet you."

Elizabeth blinked, astonished. "Me?" she asked.

Rosie nodded solemnly and leaned closer. "I have to talk to you alone, if that's okay."

"About what?" Caitlin demanded.

Rosie gave her a withering sideways glance and turned back to Elizabeth. "Listen, both of our boyfriends are neck-deep in something nasty. Maybe if you and I put our heads together, we can help them out."

Elizabeth hesitated, unsure of what to do, or think. Her gut was warning her to get as far away as possible from this girl. But her brain reminded her that it wouldn't hurt to listen to what Rosie Shaw had to say. After all, her boyfriend was in as much trouble as Todd was. Maybe she wanted the same thing as most of the other girls did—peace.

"Okay," Elizabeth said finally.

"Come on, then," Rosie said, jumping to her feet. "Let's go for a walk."

Chapter 5

Jessica and Christian emerged from the water, still laughing, and collapsed onto their beach towels. Jessica stretched out on her stomach and closed her eyes. She took a deep breath of salty air, wishing she could hold on to this moment forever.

Christian leaned over her and kissed her shoulders, sending delightful shivers up and down her spine. "Now I remember what I said," he whispered.

Jessica opened her eyes and propped her head up, with her chin resting on her folded arms. "Oh yeah? You mean I don't have to throw you in again?"

He chuckled softly and kissed her again. "You talk tough, Jessica, but you're very, very soft." He sat up and leaned forward, bracing his elbows on his raised knees. "You really do have a shot at the surfing competition," he said, his tone serious now. "I can't believe how good you've gotten."

Jessica flipped over onto her back. "I've had a great coach," she said, pulling him down for a kiss.

"Mmmm," he murmured close to her lips, "you taste good, too."

She smiled. "I just love that in a man."

"What?" he asked.

"Never-ending compliments."

"Oh do you?" he said with a laugh. "Well, before you let it all go to your head, there are some weak points you're going to have to work on before the competition."

With a sigh, she pushed herself up to a sitting position. "Okay, let me have the bad news."

He draped his arm across her shoulders and leaned his head toward hers. "I've noticed you tend to take off too soon. After you feel the first pull of the wave, you should paddle ahead two strokes to be sure you're down in the face of the wave."

Jessica nodded thoughtfully. "Yeah, I know. But there's so much to remember."

Christian hugged her close to his side. "It's like driving a car. When you first start out, you're struggling to remember a million details. Then it clicks and everything comes together."

"I wish surfing were as easy as driving," Jessica protested.

"Surfing is an art," he said. "Every wave is different

and it takes experience to be able to judge the best wave, the best moment, the best move . . . But I'm telling you, Jessica, you are *good*. You have a natural style and," he said, nibbling her neck, "you're fearless."

"You think so?" she asked, tipping her head to give him better access.

"Yeah. I figured that much out the first time I saw you, that morning when you lost your board and washed up on the shore like a beached dolphin. You were either the bravest girl I'd ever seen or the craziest."

She pushed at him playfully. "I suppose you didn't enjoy playing the big hero, rescuing my surfboard like you did."

"It was the luckiest day of my life."

She hugged him, recalling the thrilling moment when she had looked up to see him standing over her. "Mine, too."

Christian leaned back and looked into her eyes. "Tell me, Jessica, if you had known who I was from the very start, would you have come back the next morning?"

She turned away and gazed at the shimmering horizon, considering her answer. "I don't know." She turned back to him, hoping he could read the sincerity in her eyes. "I really don't, Christian. But it doesn't matter now, does it? We're together and that's what's important."

He nodded and kissed her.

"It seemed like such a fun game," Jessica said, "keeping our outside lives far away from our own special world. You were my mysterious, handsome stranger and our relationship was nothing but romance, fun, and surfing."

"And now?" he asked.

She wrapped her arms around his neck. "And now I'm so in love with you, it doesn't matter who you are out there."

"It does to me, Jessica. I've told you before, when I'm with you, I can be the person I want to be. I'm not proud of who I was. I've spent my whole life trying to prove how tough I am in order to compete with Jason. But you've shown me that I can change."

Jessica smiled softly. Christian had once confided in her how hard it was to live in the shadow of Jason, his "perfect" older brother. "I sometimes do things I'm not exactly proud of for the same reason," Jessica admitted. "Elizabeth isn't an easy act to follow, either. She makes being good seem so easy. You wouldn't catch her doing something as wicked as skipping classes to go surfing with a gorgeous hunk."

Christian laughed. "You think I'm gorgeous, huh?"

"Yeah, I do." Then she added, "But it's nice having a twin sister. I know I can count on Elizabeth to be there for me if I need her."

They held hands and sat quietly for a few moments, enjoying the warm, peaceful feeling of being together.

"By the way," Christian said, "thanks for not asking the obvious."

Jessica frowned. "What do you mean?"

"Why I joined a gang. I get asked that a lot. My parents, teachers, a long line of fancy psychologists—they all scratch their heads and look down at me as though I'm less than human."

Jessica squeezed his hand as her eyes filled with tears.

Christian continued. "I guess the gang made me believe I was somebody. I feel like such a loser compared to the rest of my family because I've never been able to measure up to their high standards."

Jessica hugged him. "Well, let me tell you something, Christian. My standards are very high and I think you measure up just fine."

"Like I said. Meeting you was the luckiest thing that ever happened to me." He wrapped his arms around her and pulled her close for a heart-stopping kiss that left Jessica breathless.

"So," he whispered, "is it less romantic now that I'm not your mysterious, handsome stranger?"

She placed her finger on her cheek and pretended to consider the question. "It's hard to say. I think we need to conduct further testing. . . ." She leaned closer and kissed him again.

"Well?" he asked when the kiss ended.

She flashed him a coy grin and shrugged. "Still don't have the answer," she said, teasing. "I'm afraid this is going to take a lot more research."

"Whatever you say," he whispered, lowering his lips to the side of her neck.

Jessica sighed wistfully. "If only we could go out together in public," she said. "I'm so proud of you, Christian. I want the whole world to know that you're mine and I'm yours."

"I know," he said. He held her close, resting his chin on top of her head. "Don't worry, surfer girl. It'll be like that when the SVH-PH War is over."

"When do you think that will be?"

"Soon," he assured her. "Very soon."

"I'm just afraid you'll be pulled into the violence against your will," she said.

He shook his head. "That won't happen. I gave you my promise I would never fight again. As long as no one at Palisades High finds out about us until this mess blows over, we'll be okay." He sighed and Jessica felt his hands tremble.

"I guess it's a good thing that the SVH students and PH students aren't on speaking terms," she said.

"Yeah, it is. Because if word gets around at Palisades High that I'm crazy about a Sweet Valley High cheerleader, there'll be trouble. *Big* trouble."

❊   ❊   ❊

"So, what's your position on this whole mess, Elizabeth?" Rosie Shaw asked as the two girls slowly circled the Palisades High track.

"I really want the war to end," Elizabeth said vehemently. "It's destroying our lives. One of my closest friends has a broken nose, and my boyfriend was arrested."

"I know what you mean," Rosie said. "I've stayed out of things till now. But I can't ignore it anymore, not after Greg got arrested and had to spend Saturday night in jail. It's not right for me to sit back and watch. I have to take an active role. After all, if we aren't part of the solution, we are the problem."

Elizabeth stopped and turned to Rosie. "You're absolutely right. That's exactly how I feel. We have to do something."

Rosie grunted in agreement. "The guys don't seem to be doing such a good job of handling things, do they?"

Elizabeth nodded. "Todd is mad at me because I won't cheer him on." She felt uncomfortable having said that because it sounded as though she was being disloyal to Todd.

"But you care a lot about him, don't you?" Rosie asked softly.

Elizabeth smiled, pleased that Rosie understood. "Yes, I do," Elizabeth answered. "Todd and I have been together for a long time. That's why this ordeal is so painful. It's coming between us."

"I feel the same way," Rosie said. "It kills me to see what this is doing to Greg. That's why I'm stepping in."

Elizabeth nodded, realizing that she and Rosie weren't so different from each other. She guardedly admitted to herself that she might have been all wrong about her.

"I know you've been trying," Rosie said. "I'm just sorry that the Palisades-Sweet Valley dance and the favorable stories about us in your school paper haven't worked. I was telling the truth before when I said I liked your articles in *The Oracle*. It must be great to be able to write so well."

"I enjoy it," Elizabeth said.

"I've tried a few times . . . short stories, poems." Rosie shook her head. "I stink at it, I'm afraid. It seems that when I get my ideas down on paper, they turn into garbage."

Elizabeth chuckled. "That's a good way to put it."

"What do you mean?" Rosie asked. "Does that happen to you, too?"

"All the time," Elizabeth said. "I guess I've learned not to worry about it if my first drafts come out badly. I do a lot of revising."

Rosie looked genuinely surprised. "Really?" she said.

"Oh sure," Elizabeth replied. "I don't think anyone can just sit down and write perfectly.

Sometimes I revise my articles three or four times before I even come close to getting them right."

"I can't believe it," Rosie said. "Your articles are so smooth and natural, I figured they were easy for you to write."

Elizabeth shook her head. "No way," she said.

"I once tried writing something for the *Palisades Pentagon*, but Marla sent it back with a nasty note telling me to stick to surfing," Rosie said.

Elizabeth gasped. "That's terrible."

Rosie shrugged. "It hurt my feelings because the article was sort of personal. It was about my Danish grandmother, how we celebrate holidays, stuff like that. I didn't think it was so bad. But maybe it was."

"I'd love to read it," Elizabeth said.

"I ripped it up and threw it away."

Elizabeth smiled sympathetically. "You deserve a lot of credit for trying and I hope you don't give up."

"Thanks, but I'm going to take Marla's advice and stick to what I'm good at," Rosie said. "She's probably right."

"I wouldn't be so sure about that," Elizabeth countered. "No one can tell what another person's potential is."

"Why would Marla cast my story aside if it didn't stink?" Rosie asked.

Elizabeth frowned, dismayed that Marla would have treated Rosie so callously, even if the piece *had* stunk. "I don't know. But don't let her or anyone else stop you from trying."

"Thanks," Rosie said with a shy grin.

"I mean it," Elizabeth said. "We'd love to have you write an article for *The Oracle*."

Rosie frowned. "Gee, I don't know," she said. "What if I truly am a horrible writer?"

Marla's thoughtlessness really did a job eroding Rosie's self-confidence, Elizabeth thought. "I'm sure you're not," she said. "I'll be glad to help you revise it if you'd like."

"You will? That's so nice of you. Well, gee. Maybe I will give writing another shot," Rosie said. "Although I have a feeling I'd cringe—or throw up—if I ever dug out my old poetry folder."

Elizabeth smiled encouragingly. "Then again, you might be pleasantly surprised."

"I don't know about that," Rosie said, shaking her head. "I'm no Christina Rossetti, that's for sure."

"Christina Rossetti is my favorite poet," Elizabeth said, surprised.

"Oh, really?" Rosie said. "Mine, too." She turned to Elizabeth with a measuring look. "You're nothing like your sister, are you?"

Elizabeth laughed. "No, I'm not."

"Did you know that I'm going to be competing against Jessica in the Rock TV surfing competition?" Rosie asked.

"Yes, she told me." Thinking about Jessica made Elizabeth feel uncomfortable all of a sudden.

"I know a set of twins who are exactly alike, right down to their favorite flavor of ice cream," Rosie said. "It's great that you and Jessica have been able to maintain your individuality."

That is the understatement of the year, Elizabeth thought. "Yes," she said, "we certainly have."

"It's so easy to talk with you, Elizabeth," Rosie said. "I really feel I can trust you."

Elizabeth took the compliment to heart. She considered trust to be one of the most important bonds between people. She reminded herself never to judge a book by its cover because apparently she'd figured Rosie all wrong.

"Jessica is going out with Ken Matthews, the Gladiators' football captain, isn't she?" Rosie asked. "The one who fumbled the ball during the big game?"

"Jessica." Elizabeth sighed uneasily. "If our boyfriends are neck-deep in trouble, my sister is in up to her eyebrows."

"Why, what's wrong?" Rosie asked.

Elizabeth hesitated, wondering if she should reveal what she knew. She wasn't entirely sure how much she trusted Rosie Shaw. *But if Rosie trusts me*, Elizabeth thought, *then maybe I should also make the effort*. Besides, if they could work together to put an end to the SVH-PH rivalry, Jessica would be the happiest one of all. "Jessica has been secretly seeing Christian Gorman," Elizabeth said.

Rosie lifted her eyebrows, but said nothing. Elizabeth continued. "It started out innocently enough between them. He was giving her surfing lessons. But things just sort of grew out of hand, according to Jessica. Anyway, Ken found out about them a few days ago and now the SVH guys are turning it into one more reason to hate Palisades High." Elizabeth shook her head. "As if they didn't have enough to stir them up already."

"What do you think the SVH guys will do in retaliation?" Rosie asked.

"Who knows?" Elizabeth answered. "I hate to think about it."

Rosie looked away. "We'll have to figure something out before they have a chance to move against us—I mean, against the PH guys. Will you tell me if you hear anything?"

Elizabeth nodded. "Of course."

"Do they usually meet at that warehouse where the fight was Saturday night?" Rosie asked.

Elizabeth shrugged. "I don't really know. Todd and the others have been pretty mysterious about what they've been doing."

"Well, don't you worry about a thing," Rosie said. "I'll figure out a way to put an end to all this nonsense, once and for all." She stopped walking and turned to Elizabeth. "I have to be going now," Rosie said. "I'm glad we talked, Elizabeth."

Elizabeth smiled. "Me, too."

"I'll give you a call as soon as I come up with a concrete plan," Rosie said. "And you call me if you find out what the SVH guys' next move is."

"I'll do that," Elizabeth replied.

Rosie grinned. "See ya." Then she turned and jogged in the direction of the parking lot.

As Elizabeth walked toward the bleachers to rejoin her friends, she felt as though a burden had been lifted from her shoulders. She'd found a powerful ally.

Rosie was going to come to the rescue.

Elizabeth lay in her bed that evening, staring at the ceiling. Although she barely slept at all the night before, she felt too keyed up to relax. Premonitions of disaster floated through her mind, almost against her will. Giving up trying to chase them away, she tossed off the covers and rolled out of bed. Hoping that a swim would calm her jittery nerves, she slipped on her green maillot swimsuit and headed outside to the family pool.

Jessica was already there, drifting around the pool on an inflatable raft with a dreamy look on her face. Elizabeth dropped her towel on a deck chair and jumped in. She swam laps as hard as she could, hoping the exertion would tire her out enough to sleep.

By the time she pulled herself out of the water, her muscles felt like overcooked spaghetti and her mind was blissfully silent. "That felt great," she murmured as she picked up her towel and sat down on the edge of the pool. A nice hot shower and a cup of herbal tea would probably be all she needed to send herself into a deep, restful sleep.

Jessica turned to her with a wistful smile. "Christian thinks I have a shot at winning the up-coming Rock TV surfing competition, did I tell you?"

Elizabeth wrapped the towel around her shoulders. "Yes, you did," she said. "Twice."

Jessica sighed. "He's such a great teacher, so patient and gentle. He makes me feel as if I can do anything. Even if I wasn't madly in love with him, I'd still love him."

"That doesn't make sense," Elizabeth said.

Jessica giggled. "It's hard to make sense of anything right now. I guess the only thing that matters is that he and I are so perfect for each other." Jessica sat up, causing the raft to dip below the water line. "It's so great to be able to talk to some-body about him at last. You can't imagine how hard it was to keep him a secret. He's such a wonderful guy. I wish I could tell the whole world about him."

Elizabeth yawned. She tried to listen with some degree of interest, but Jessica had been going on and on about how gorgeous, witty, smart, talented, awesome, wonderful, and marvelous Christian Gorman was ever since she got home. Elizabeth rubbed the towel through her soaking hair and wrapped it in a turban around her head.

"Have you ever felt anything like that?" Jessica was saying, catching Elizabeth off guard. "It's as though you're being chased by this huge beast and instead of cowering, you stand up to him and ride on his back."

Elizabeth frowned. "Christian chases you and gives you piggyback rides? That sounds awfully strange."

"No, Lizzie!" Jessica said, splashing water over Elizabeth's legs. "I was talking about the wave, silly. Riding the wave. It's an incredible experience. Although Christian says the surfer doesn't ride the wave; the wave rides the surfer. When he and I are in the ocean together, it's like our own alternate world where nothing can touch us." Jessica grinned. "I can't wait to beat that Rosie Shaw."

"I met her," Elizabeth began, intending to tell Jessica about the conversation she'd had with Rosie that afternoon.

Jessica cut her off. "I can't stand that girl," she said with a shudder. "She said I didn't have what it takes to become a surfer, but I'm going to make her eat those words." She grinned. "And it's going to be so much fun."

Elizabeth snapped her mouth shut. Maybe it wasn't such a good idea to mention that she and Rosie were teaming up to end the school rivalry.

"I still feel badly about Ken though," Jessica said. "I should have been honest with him, or at least broken up with him sooner."

Elizabeth nodded in agreement. "It would have saved him a lot of mental anguish. He's been through so much these last few days, wondering what was going on with you and worrying about you when you didn't show up at school."

"Oh, I know," Jessica said. "I hated having to sneak around behind his back. We still have to sneak around, as far as Palisades High goes. Christian says if anyone there finds out about him and me, things will definitely explode. As long as they don't know, there's hope that we can end the war."

Elizabeth gulped, wondering if she'd blown it by telling Rosie. But then she recalled the sweet, concerned expression on Rosie's face and assured herself that her new friend could be trusted.

The cordless phone on the patio table rang. Elizabeth got up and answered it.

"Hi, Elizabeth. It's Rosie."

Elizabeth glanced at Jessica in the pool, then turned away. "Yes, hello."

"I have a brilliant idea," Rosie said. "Meet me tomorrow at noon." She gave Elizabeth the directions to a restaurant that was near Palisades High. "You can't miss it," Rosie added. "It's on the left-hand side of the road. Look for a long, narrow shack with the ugliest paint job you've ever seen. And don't worry. It might not look like much, but trust me, the food is great."

"Sounds good," Elizabeth said, forcing her voice to sound casual and cheerful. "I'll see you then."

"Who was that?" Jessica asked when Elizabeth returned to the pool.

Elizabeth nervously caught her bottom lip between her teeth. "It was . . . Caitlin," she answered, feeling her face grow warm. Then she pulled the towel off her head, dropped it on the ground and jumped into the pool for another set of laps.

Chapter 6

The next morning, Todd arrived at school earlier than usual and headed straight for the *Oracle* office. Elizabeth had been giving him the cold shoulder for the past twenty-four hours and he couldn't take it another minute. With the stress of being arrested and facing his court hearing, which was scheduled for that afternoon, he'd reached his limit of endurance. The stone wall between him and Elizabeth was more than he could stand.

He peered inside the room, but Elizabeth hadn't arrived yet, so he waited for her in the hall. His palms were damp and his heart pounded as if he were running for his life.

He held his breath when he first spotted her walking toward him. She was wearing a black pair of those clingy, stretchy legging things, which showed off her gorgeous legs, and a long, soft pink sweater. The only jewelry she wore was the gold lavaliere that her parents had given her, and a watch. A feeling of tenderness came over him. She moved with natural elegance, the most beautiful girl he could imagine.

As she came closer, Todd stepped forward and cleared his throat. "Hi," he said, softly. Elizabeth walked right by as if she hadn't seen him. Todd's heart fell, crushed. "Elizabeth," he said. Then again, louder, "Elizabeth!"

She stopped and turned around, to his utter relief. "What is it?"

He took a step closer to her. "We have to talk, Liz."

"I thought you weren't interested in talking to me," she said. "Last I heard, I stabbed you in the back."

Todd's gaze skidded away nervously, then returned to her face. "I'm sorry for what I said. I was furious at you for calling the police and getting me arrested. But after I'd had a chance to cool down, I realized you were only doing what you thought was right. I know you would never do anything to intentionally hurt me."

Elizabeth's eyes filled with tears. "I was so afraid, Todd. Afraid something terrible would happen."

"I know." Todd took another step toward her. "I was so scared in jail, I just wanted to crawl in a hole and hide. I feel like my whole life is falling apart. Yesterday, I spent forty minutes in the office, listening to Chrome Dome Cooper telling me how badly I've 'disappointed' him—as if hurting the principal's feelings should be my biggest worry right now. Coach Tilman is threatening to have me kicked off the basketball team and Mrs. Green wants me to come to the guidance office to discuss my options in case I blow my chances for an athletic scholarship. You wouldn't believe how upset my parents are. I don't know if we'll ever get past this disaster." His throat tightened with emotions, choking off his words. He swallowed hard and said, "I really need you, Elizabeth, especially right now during this tough time."

She looked at him with a watery smile and reached out her arms. "I need you too, Todd."

He took her into his arms and hugged her tightly, feeling his heart swell with gladness. "I've missed you so much," he whispered. "Those guys have really messed up our lives. Now do you understand why we have to get back at Palisades High? We can't just let them get away with what they've done to us."

Suddenly Elizabeth stepped out of his arms. Without another word, she walked away. Todd watched her go, realizing for the hundredth time that women just didn't understand what it was like to be a guy.

°   °   °

Later that morning, as Elizabeth was getting ready to leave the school building for her meeting with Rosie, she spotted Mr. Fellows walking down the hall in her direction. Hoping he hadn't already seen her, she ducked into the girls' room to hide. She was planning to skip his class that afternoon, along with a few others.

Elizabeth slumped against one of the sinks, her heart beating rapidly. "I can't believe I'm doing this," she whispered. Skipping classes might not be a big deal to her sister, but to Elizabeth it was unthinkable. Especially today, when she would be missing a unit exam in science and a mock trial in history.

Meeting Rosie was more important, though. Todd's attitude that morning helped convince Elizabeth that drastic action was necessary to end the SVH-PH War. Even after being arrested, he was ready to jump right back into the same mess that had put him in jail in the first place. Rosie was right— their boyfriends were in it neck-deep and sinking fast.

Elizabeth only hoped that it wasn't too late to warn Rosie not to tell anyone at Palisades High about Jessica and Christian. Elizabeth would have mentioned it on the phone when Rosie had called the night before if Jessica hadn't been within earshot.

A moment later, Elizabeth peeked into the hall. Finding it empty, she hurried to the side exit where she couldn't be seen from the windows in the main office. Outside, she ran as fast as she could to the Jeep. When she started the engine, her guilty conscience made the sound seem unusually loud.

Following the directions Rosie had given her, Elizabeth found herself on a twisting road which seemed to lead nowhere. The last building she'd passed was at least two miles back. Something didn't seem right, she thought. It was possible that she'd made a wrong turn somewhere along the way, or . . .

She didn't want to consider the possibility that this might be another Palisades High trap, but after what had happened to Winston, she couldn't prevent her suspicions. Maybe she'd been too quick to trust Rosie.

Suddenly there it was: the Silverhead Diner, exactly as Rosie had described. And the paint job was terrible, Elizabeth noticed. It looked as though someone had come up with the clever idea of spray-painting the entire building in metallic silver, but never got around to finishing the job. There were streaks of bare, weathered wood peeking out from between the fuzzy edged bands of silver, with drips and blotches of color here and there. But after worrying so much, Elizabeth thought the building looked beautiful.

She parked the Jeep in the gravel parking lot and went inside. The interior decor wasn't a whole lot better than the exterior. Two rows of orange booths lined the long dining area, most of them empty. The smell of grease hung heavily in the air.

Rosie was already there, sitting in a back booth with a plate of French fries on the table in front of her. Elizabeth rushed over to her and blurted, "Have you told anyone about Jessica and Christian?"

Rosie looked at her with an amused expression. "Is that how people greet each other at Sweet Valley High?" she asked.

"I'm sorry," Elizabeth said, slipping into the other side of the booth. The vinyl seat cover was torn and a jagged edge caught a thread of her knitted leggings, snagging them. "I'm afraid this mess is getting the best of me," she said, shifting to find a comfortable spot. "It's as though my whole life is falling apart."

"That's okay," Rosie said. "I understand. And no, I haven't told anyone about Romeo and Juliet."

Elizabeth leaned back and exhaled a sigh of relief. "Please don't. Jessica thinks there'll be even more trouble if anyone at Palisades High finds out about her and Christian."

"I don't think we have to worry about those two," Rosie said. "We'll take good care of them. By the way, I hope you don't mind that I went ahead and ordered without waiting for you. My free period ends in twenty minutes and I can't miss my next class. We're reviewing for a big test tomorrow."

Elizabeth winced, reminded of the classes she was skipping herself. A waitress stopped at the table to take Elizabeth's order. Elizabeth realized she wasn't very hungry and ordered a glass of orange juice. The waitress walked away grumbling about cheapskates filling up the booths in her station.

"Don't mind her," Rosie said. "They have to be rude. It's part of the Silverhead's charm. Anyway, what are Todd's plans for tonight?"

Elizabeth shrugged. "I don't know. We're not exactly on speaking terms right now. My guess is that the guys will be holed up somewhere, grumbling about the girls. The Sweet Valley High girls have initiated a no-dates policy. We're completely giving up our boyfriends until they come to their senses and put an end to the fighting."

Rose looked at her incredulously. "That's wild! How did you come up with that idea?"

Elizabeth had given that question some thought on her own. "It must have been from reading *Lysistrata* in my English class. It's a Greek play written over two thousand years ago about some women who refused to have any contact with their husbands and boyfriends until the men stopped fighting a war. Except Aristophanes wrote it as a comedy, but so far no one at SVH is laughing."

Rosie's jaw dropped. "I love it. And it fits in perfectly with my plan." She leaned forward and dropped her voice, as if she were disclosing a top-secret military maneuver. "First, we'll get each group of guys together. Then you and I will go to one group with the message that the other one wants peace. After we've convinced them, we'll go to the other group and tell them the exact same thing. If both sides believe the other one gave up first, all of the guys will be able to walk away with their pride intact."

"That's a great idea," Elizabeth said, amazed at the simple brilliance.

"Can you find out where the Sweet Valley High guys will be meeting tonight?" Rosie asked.

"Oh sure," Elizabeth said enthusiastically. "I'll sweet-talk Todd into telling me. I think a few white lies are perfectly justified in this case," she said. "After all, if the plan works, we'll finally be able to bring an end to this madness."

Rosie grinned. "That's right, Elizabeth. An end to the madness."

"What about the Palisades High guys? Are they planning to get together tonight?"

Rosie picked up a French fry and dragged it through a puddle of ketchup on her plate. Then she popped it into her mouth and licked her fingers. "You leave them to me," she said. "I'll handle Greg and the Palisades High guys."

As Todd drove to the courthouse after school, the fear of losing his freedom consumed him. Several of the guys had wished him luck and offered moral support, but their encouragement seemed hollow now that he was actually on the way to his hearing. Frightening questions shot through his mind. Would this be his last day as a free person? What kind of future did he have in store? Todd thought of the big plans he had for his life. What were his chances of winning a basketball scholarship and attending a good college now that he was a violent criminal?

Elizabeth had been right all along. The rivalry between Sweet Valley and Palisades had to stop. Trying to get back at PH would only force them to get back at SVH. It no longer mattered who had started the trouble; the important thing now was ending it. Once and for all.

If only Elizabeth were with him. She made the tough times bearable. He recalled the image of her walking away from him that morning and was tortured by the thought that it might turn out to be the last time he'd ever see her.

The sound of screeching tires and blaring horns shocked him alert. He realized he'd just run a red light at a busy intersection and had narrowly missed causing a huge accident. "Come on!" he said to himself aloud, shaken. "How many stupid mistakes is one guy allowed?"

As Todd turned down the final block and approached his dreaded destination, his stomach began to flutter nervously. The Sweet Valley

Courthouse was a sprawling, Colonial-type building surrounded by well-manicured lawns and flower beds. But despite its polished facade, to Todd it looked like a haunted castle of unspeakable horror. His heart thumped wildly as he got out of the car.

He vowed that if the judge was lenient with him, he'd make up for all of the recent lunacy. And the first step he'd take would be to beg Elizabeth's forgiveness—right after he went to Bruce's house and tried to convince the rest of the guys to end the fighting. Surely he could make them see that the whole rivalry was going nowhere.

Jessica arrived at the beach that afternoon nearly an hour late and in a foul mood. Elizabeth had demanded that Jessica drive her home after school, pointing out that the Jeep belonged to both of them. Then, for the entire duration of the ride, Elizabeth had alternated between whining about how worried she felt about Todd's court hearing and snipping at Jessica's driving. *Something is going on with my sister*, Jessica thought. Elizabeth didn't lose her cool very easily, or often—but when she did, it wasn't a pretty sight.

Christian's blue van was the only car in the small municipal parking lot. Seeing it there, like an old friend, filled her with joy and drove away all of the grumbling irritation she'd been dragging along with her. She never would have guessed that the mere sight of a Volkswagen could lift a person's spirits so quickly and completely.

The sun was beginning to set, making their world seem magical. The beach was deserted except for Christian, who was sitting a few yards away, a lone figure against the backdrop of shimmering blue ocean and a hazy pink sky. *He is so beautiful*, she thought as she stood back, marveling at the scene before her. He looked like the statue of a Greek hero carved in marble.

As though he sensed her presence behind him, he turned. His eyes brightened and he flashed her a welcoming smile. She ran to him and threw her arms around his shoulders. He smelled of salty ocean waves and sea breezes. This was no statue of stone, she thought, stroking his chest. His skin was warm and his heart thumped as wildly as her own.

"What did I do before I met you, surfer girl?" Christian whispered against her ear. "Seems like I've known you forever."

"Me, too," Jessica said.

They held each other for a long moment, reminding Jessica of how lucky she was to have him in her life. "Why don't we skip the lesson today?" she said. "It's late and I've been working so hard. I deserve a break, don't you agree?"

He leaned back and faced her. "I agree you deserve the best surfing instruction you can get. Are you feeling tired?"

"Yes," she answered.

"Great. Then we'll work on wipeouts again," he said.

She opened her eyes wide and glared at him. "What are you talking about? I said I was tired."

"I know," he said. "It's best to practice in conditions that will be as close as possible to the real event. You have to be able to wipe out safely, even when you're exhausted."

"Christian Gorman, you are no fun at all. I don't even know why I like you."

He grinned. "Because you think I'm a gorgeous hunk, remember?"

She shook her head, teasing him with a blank stare. "No, I don't remember."

"I know just the thing to refresh your memory," he said with threatening smile. "I learned it from a real genius."

Jessica sighed wearily and nestled her face against his neck. "You're a slave driver."

"And you're the surfer who's going to walk away with the Rock TV all-state trophy," Christian said. "So quit your bellyaching, darlin', and listen to your coach. The more comfortable you feel about failing, the more secure you'll be at winning. Knowing how to wipe out safely will make you a more confident surfer. You'll lose that desperation to stay up during the ride and be free to focus on balance and style. And who knows, it might help save that pretty neck of yours," he added, cupping his hands around her chin. He lowered his lips and planted a big wet kiss on the side of her neck.

"But we already went over it," Jessica complained. "I'm supposed to do a duck-dive to the bottom and stay down so I won't get caught in the current."

"That's just for starters. And besides, there's a big difference between reciting what you learned and *knowing* it. Your whole body has to learn the techniques and that means practice, lots and lots of practice."

Jessica grumbled as they carried their boards to the water, but only because she refused to give in too easily. To herself she admitted that Christian's logic made perfect sense. Whenever she would wipe out, she always relied on him to help her. But she couldn't expect Christian to be standing by to rescue her forever. If she wiped out during a competition, she'd have to save herself.

"The first thing to remember is: *Don't panic*," he said as they paddled out to meet the waves. "You're going to have some important, split-second decisions to make and it's much easier to think straight when you're calm."

"Okay, gotcha. Stay calm," Jessica said.

He flashed her a wicked grin. "Glad you're listening, surfer girl."

Pretending to be daydreaming, she turned to him and blinked. "Oh, did you just say something?" she asked.

He tipped his head back and laughed. "You're too much, Jessica."

"Yes, but enough about me," she said, flashing him a saucy grin. "We have work to do, coach."

"And you're so cute, too," he added. "Okay, back to the lesson. Pay attention. Let's say you're up on your board and you start to lose control. If you're riding a wave that isn't too big, you might be able to drop to your stomach and ride prone until you straighten off. In any case, you should try to hold on to your board. If it's not possible, then dive off the front or back. Don't ever go off on the shore side because the wave will push the board into you, and you run the risk of getting hit on the head."

"I guess I was pretty lucky that first day." She smiled and winked at him. "For lots of reasons."

He winked back at her. "I like to think so. Anyway, keep in mind that the average time under water in a wipeout is only five to ten seconds. It may seem longer because you usually won't have a chance to take a deep breath, and then of course, the wave will knock some of the wind out of you. That's why it's important to stay calm and focused so you won't be taken by surprise and can use those last few seconds to fill your lungs."

Jessica nodded. "My lungs felt as if they were on fire by the time I surfaced."

He turned to her with a look of pure admiration. "And you didn't give up on surfing," he said.

She smiled, feeling as if she were glowing. "Of course not," she said. "I had to impress this gorgeous hunk I'd just met."

"And you did," he said.

They paddled a bit farther. "Okay, this is far enough," Christian said. The waves were nearly eight feet high. Jessica studied their procession as they lifted and lowered her surfboard like a roller coaster. Christian paddled his board closer to her. "Are you nervous?" he asked.

She turned to him and nodded. "I always am at this point, just as I realize what I'm about to do."

He chuckled. "Me, too. That's what makes it fun."

Jessica laughed. Of course he would know exactly how she felt. He was her soul mate, after all.

"We'll ride for a few feet and when I give the signal, take it to mean that you're just beginning to lose your footing. Remember not to panic, especially when you hit the water. Give yourself a few seconds to become oriented. When you feel the wave let up, swim to the surface, and immediately check for the next wave. You don't want to be surprised by another wave crashing over your head as you take your first gasp."

A promising wave rolled toward her. Jessica positioned herself for takeoff and slowly stood up, balancing with her arms. As she'd come to expect, her fear lost its grip and was replaced with a tremendous surge of ecstasy. She was flying, the wind whipping her hair. Then she heard Christian's loud whistle. With a groan, she prepared herself for the crash.

By the time the lesson was over, Jessica figured she had swallowed and inhaled enough ocean water to drown an elephant. She learned two things she hadn't known before: how to control her fear of wiping out and that seaweed actually came in different flavors—all of them bad.

Christian was beaming at her as they snuggled together on their beach towels. "You've got what it takes, Jessica. I'm going to be so proud of you when you win that trophy."

Jessica's complaints seemed unimportant all of a sudden as she wrapped her arms around him. Christian's glowing praise made everything worthwhile. She decided she'd gladly eat a ton of seaweed for this reward.

Christian began idly scooping sand and pushing it into a mound. Jessica joined him and the pile of sand soon became an elaborate sand castle. Like two very serious children, they worked industriously on their project. Jessica once again marveled at how it felt both exciting and comfortable to be with Christian.

The sun set lower and the sky turned to bright orange. When the castle was finished, they stepped back and proudly admired their creation. Its six towers were decorated with flags of green seaweed and chipped shells outlined the windows and doors. Christian turned and gazed into Jessica's eyes. "Someday, you and I will live in a house like this."

Jessica nodded, meeting the promise in his smoky blue eyes. "Yes, I know." And with those words, she realized that something special had just passed between them. Their commitment to each other was solid now and it would last forever.

They held each other for a long time. "I swear I'll always love you, surfer girl," Christian whispered close to her ear.

"I'll always love you too, coach."

He pulled back, holding Jessica's shoulders. There was an intensity in his eyes which she'd never seen before. "No matter what happens, Jessica, you and I will always be together."

She raised her hand and gently touched his lips. "Forever," she whispered, moving in for another kiss.

Chapter 7

Todd squirmed in his seat, a hard wooden bench which was becoming unbearable. There were several cases ahead of his and the waiting was killing him. The judge was an elderly woman who looked like the kind, grandmotherly type. But Todd soon discovered that despite her soft, white hair and rosy cheeks, she had the heart of a wicked witch.

His father was seated on one side of him and the lawyer his parents had hired was seated on the other. Neither one of them looked too hopeful as they stared straight ahead with solemn expressions.

Todd gulped as he listened to the judge pass another stiff sentence, this time to a man who had driven away from a self-serve filling station without paying for his gas. If she felt any compassion at all, she hid it well. Todd felt himself getting more and more nervous by the second.

He imagined the judge handing him a life sentence, dooming him to spend the rest of his days in a cold cell, surrounded by people with stern faces. Maybe they'd lock him up in a windowless box by himself. What did they feed guys in solitary confinement? *Cold, greasy broth and moldy bread,* he mused. And they'd serve it through a slot in the thick, steel door. He might go months before seeing another human being.

Suddenly he heard his name called out. He was supposed to stand, but his body refused to move. His father grabbed his arm and pulled him to his feet.

With his legs shaking, Todd walked through the low wooden gate which separated the spectators from the action. The judge held up a sheet of paper and read off the list of crimes: "Three counts of aggravated assault, vandalism, disturbing the peace, trespassing, striking an officer, destruction of property, battery . . ."

Todd stared at her in disbelief. Was she actually accusing him of *all that*? he wondered. *There has to be some mistake,* his mind screamed. Only a truly bad—or deranged—person would do those terrible things.

When she was finished reading the charges, the judge leaned forward and looked Todd in the eye.

"Well, young man, what do you have to say for yourself?"

One thing he couldn't say was that the accusations were false—because they were completely true. The realization struck him right in the face. He had committed each and every crime on the list.

"Perhaps you didn't hear me, Mr. Wilkins," she said in a cold, shrill voice. "I asked you a question."

"Um . . . er . . . your . . . um, honor . . ." His throat squeezed, choking off his stuttering reply. At that point, Todd would have thrown himself on the floor and begged for mercy if he weren't frozen solid with fear and shock.

She fixed him with a piercing glare. "This case clearly exemplifies a major problem facing our world today—the mistaken belief, so prevalent among our youth, that one's affiliations give just cause to the perpetration of violence . . ."

Todd stood perfectly still, hardly breathing, as the judge continued her stern lecture.

". . . Therefore, young man, I'm sentencing you to thirty hours of community service and I hope I never see you in my courtroom again."

Todd blinked, wondering if he'd heard right. *Thirty hours of community service?* He wasn't going to jail! His body felt limp with relief. He looked at his father and saw the same relief on his face. As they left the courthouse, Todd felt almost happy, for the first time in days.

And he had a promise to keep to himself. He was going to do whatever it took to end the SVH-PH War.

The guys were all going to meet at Bruce's house later. Todd decided he would talk to them tonight and try to set things right. Then he'd call Elizabeth and tell her that he'd finally come to his senses. It was going to feel wonderful to be able to put the whole nightmare behind them at last.

When they reached their cars, Todd's father turned to him as if he were about to say something, but Todd spoke first. "Dad, if you're going to tell me that you hope this taught me a lesson, don't worry. It has."

Mr. Wilkins nodded. "You were very fortunate today, but I don't think you should count on being so lucky next time."

"There isn't going to be a next time," Todd promised.

"Good. Now, let's get home. Your mother is waiting anxiously, I'm sure."

"Hey, Elizabeth, what's shaking?" Rosie Shaw asked in a cheerful voice.

Holding the phone in one hand, Elizabeth paced nervously across her bedroom. "I just got through talking with Todd," she said, shifting the phone to her other ear. She'd been jittery all night in anticipation of her and Rosie's plan. "The guys will be meeting at Bruce Patman's house tonight."

"Very good. Did you tell Todd what we're up to?"

"No," Elizabeth replied. "I think it's important for all the guys to believe that the other side is ready to stop fighting."

"Good," Rosie said again. "And you really think he doesn't suspect that you're up to something?"

"Todd has a lot on his mind right now," Elizabeth said. "Besides, if he were suspicious, I'm sure he would've come right out and asked."

"Okay," Rosie said. "You know him best. So anyway, where was it they were meeting?"

"Bruce Patman's house."

"Oh, right. And where exactly is that?" Rosie asked.

"On Valley Crest Drive," Elizabeth answered.

There was a slight pause. Then Rosie asked, "Where is Valley Crest Drive?"

"Don't worry," Elizabeth said. "We're going there together, remember? I know the way to Bruce's house."

Rosie chuckled. "Of course you do, Elizabeth. I was just asking for logistical planning. You know, trying to figure out how much time it'll take to go from one place to the other."

"Oh. Well, the Patman Mansion is in the hill section of town." Elizabeth described how to get there, using Sweet Valley High as the reference point.

"So does this guy really live in a mansion?" Rosie asked.

Elizabeth dragged the phone over to a corner of her room and sat down on the floor. "Yes, it's really very nice. They have a pool and tennis courts—"

"Do they have guard dogs or anything?" Rosie asked.

"Quit worrying, Rosie," Elizabeth said. "I've known the Patmans for years. They'll let us in, trust me."

"Okay, Elizabeth." Rosie paused. "Trust is a great thing between friends, isn't it?"

Elizabeth glanced across the room. She normally kept it impeccably neat and tidy, but now she couldn't help noticing the signs of her own strained nerves here and there—papers scattered across her desk, her bathrobe lying on the floor, a stack of laundry she'd carelessly left on top of the dresser. She was overwhelmed and beginning to fall apart. Of course she trusted Rosie Shaw. She didn't have a choice. Teaming up with Rosie was the best hope they had.

"Meet me at the Silverhead Diner at nine o'-clock and we'll make our move," Rosie said.

"I might have a problem with that," Elizabeth said. "My sister and I share a car. She's got it right now and I don't know what time she'll be home.

113

Why don't we meet here at my house, instead?"

"No!" Rosie blurted. Then she added, in a calmer tone, "I mean, maybe that's not such a good idea. I'm not sure how long the Palisades High guys will be at their meeting place and if we have to drive all the way from your house, we might miss them. When does your sister usually get home?"

Elizabeth snorted. "There's no 'usual' where Jessica is concerned. She lives by her own unique clock."

"Do you know where she is?" Rosie asked.

"Somewhere with, um, Christian, I think." Elizabeth felt an uneasy stirring in her gut.

"My guess is that she'll be home in plenty of time."

"How can you be so sure?" Elizabeth asked. The uneasiness turned to dread. "I worry about her constantly because I never know what she's going to do next."

"You don't have to worry this time, Elizabeth. If she's with Christian, I'm sure he'll send her home early. In fact, I'd bet money on it. He'll want Jessica to get her beauty sleep, after all."

"Okay, if you're right I'll see you at the Silverhead Diner at nine o'clock," Elizabeth said. "If not, I'll call you."

"Don't worry!" Rosie said. "Nothing can go wrong with you and me teaming up together."

Elizabeth smiled. "I hope you're right. I have a

good feeling about this," she added, borrowing some of Rosie's confidence. "I really think your plan is going to work."

"Oh, yes," Rosie said with a laugh. "My plan is going to work very, very nicely."

Elizabeth hung up, Rosie's final words echoing in her mind. There was something . . . a puzzle, a vague thought hovering just out of reach. Elizabeth tried to think of what it might be that was gnawing at her. Suddenly the phone rang again, startling her. It was Enid.

"What's going on, Elizabeth?" Enid asked. "You sound strange. Is anything wrong?"

"I'm planning to meet Rosie Shaw in a few hours," Elizabeth answered.

"You're *what*?"

Elizabeth told Enid what she and Rosie were planning to do that night.

After a long silence, Enid said, "I don't trust her, Liz. There's something about the way she looks at a person, as if she's searching for a weak spot to sink her teeth into."

"I thought the same thing at first, until I got to know her," Elizabeth said. "She really is a nice person underneath that tough exterior. And besides, her plan is ingenious."

Enid hesitated. "I suppose if she's sincere about ending the rivalry, she can't be all that bad."

"Rosie wants the same thing we do," Elizabeth said. "If everything works out the way we've planned, we'll have peace by tomorrow."

"Okay," Enid said, "but I'm coming with you."

A cool breeze off the water put a chill in the night air. Jessica sat with her arms wrapped around her legs and her chin resting on her knees as she watched Christian walk to the van to get a blanket. *Even the way he moves is a study in beauty and form,* she thought.

She saw him removing a sheet of paper which had been stuck under his windshield wiper. He stood there studying it for a long time. Jessica wondered what it was. It was too large to be a parking ticket.

When he jogged back to her, without the blanket, his expression had turned serious, almost angry.

"What's wrong?" she asked.

"I have to go meet my friends," he said breathlessly.

Jessica felt a sinking sensation in her gut, a warning of danger. "Has something happened?"

Instead of answering, he held her close and kissed her passionately. "Will you meet me here later tonight, at midnight?" he asked.

Jessica nodded. The thought occurred to her that in the past she would never have stood for a guy walking out on her to go see his friends. Of course she'd never loved anyone as she did Christian, but it was more than that. She trusted him. If he said he had to leave, she believed him. Her only concern was for his safety.

Christian walked her to the Jeep. Before she got in, he took off his coral necklace and fastened it around her neck.

Jessica touched it reverently, her eyes filling with tears as Christian turned to go.

He started walking away, then stopped and turned back to her. "Always remember, Jessica," he said, "I'll love you forever."

"When is this going to end? When they throw the last one of us in jail?" Todd asked aloud, practicing his peace speech as he drove up the hill to the Patman Mansion. His words sounded all right in the confines of his car, but whether they'd hold up when he faced the guys was a different matter. He tried to believe that his friends would listen to him, but he was afraid his grand words were going to fall on deaf ears.

He was happy Elizabeth had called him earlier that evening. It had been such a great surprise to answer the phone and hear her voice. She'd sounded like her old sweet self and he couldn't wait to talk things over with her. But right now, his stomach was queasy with dread. He had a feeling that tonight was going to be a big night.

He jumped at the sound of someone rapping on the windshield. Ken was standing next to the car, waving frantically. "You're late, man," he said. "Some of the guys were beginning to wonder whether or not you were going to show. I told them you'd never wimp out on us." Ken pulled open the door of the car. "Come on, hurry up," he urged Todd.

"I had my court hearing today," Todd reminded him as they walked to the house. The Patman Mansion and grounds were impressive, attesting to the wealth of Bruce's family. The lush trees and gardens were professionally tended, as was the Olympic-sized swimming pool and tennis court, which was cut into the hill just below the mansion.

"Oh yeah, right," Ken said. "How did it go?"

"The judge let me off easy. I have to do thirty hours of community service."

"Eliminating those Palisades High creeps would be a great community service."

Todd took a deep breath. "Ken, about all that, I've been thinking—"

"All the guys are really steamed tonight," Ken said. "Everyone agrees we've gone too easy on those slugs. It's time to show them we're not going to take it anymore. Ricky wants them to pay in blood for the eleven stitches he had to get in his arm. You should see Bryce and Ted. They're ready to go march over to Palisades right now and crack a few skulls." Ken chuckled. "I wonder what the PH guys are saying about us right now. They think they're so tough. Greg McMullen is such a jerk. I can't stand him. And I really hate Gorman. I've never hated anyone so much in my life," he said. "I wish Christian Gorman were dead."

Todd felt his self-confidence withering. With the guys so fired up, he wondered how he was going to voice his own views without sounding like a total wimp.

At nine o'clock sharp, Elizabeth and Enid arrived at the Silverhead Diner. The gravel parking lot was crowded with motorcycles and country-western music was blaring from inside the building.

"Are you sure this place is safe?" Enid said, eyeing the dilapidated building with a dubious expression.

"We won't be here long," Elizabeth said, trying to sound reassuring while she wondered the same thing. "Rosie will be here any minute."

"I don't know about all this," Enid said. "I know you believe in her, but I'm still not convinced Rosie Shaw is on our side."

"You'll see when you get to know her," Elizabeth said, leading the way inside.

The air was thick and hazy with cigarette

smoke. There was a rougher crowd gathered at the Silverhead Diner than there had been yesterday afternoon when Elizabeth had come to meet Rosie. Most of them looked like bikers who had lived through some tough times. The dining room was a sea of black leather, steel chains, and tattoos. The women were decked out the same as the men, with the addition of thick makeup and teased hair.

Elizabeth covered her ears. The noise was deafening, with music and conversations screamed back and forth between the booths. Everyone seemed to know one another. A nasty looking guy with a red scar across his forehead whistled at her and Enid.

Another guy called out, "Fresh meat." The woman he was with slapped him across the face. He slapped her right back. Elizabeth and Enid turned to each other and exchanged looks of horror and disgust.

"Now I *know* I don't like the looks of this place," Enid whispered.

"Just try to act natural," Elizabeth whispered back.

"Oh, I am," Enid said. "This is my natural reaction when I'm scared for my life."

They carefully made their way to an empty booth next to a window so they could watch for Rosie. "So, Elizabeth," Enid began, "explain to me how you and Rosie Shaw have come to be such great friends."

Elizabeth shrugged. "I spent some time with her, that's all."

Enid rolled her eyes. "Well, they do say that politics makes for strange alliances."

"It's more than that, really," Elizabeth protested.

"If you say so," Enid said, sounding doubtful.

"No, I mean it. She has strong feelings of loyalty to her school and to the people she cares about, and I admire that. Rosie is a nice person when you get to know her."

"And you've gotten to know her very well in—what has it been—thirty hours?" Enid said.

A tall man with bloodshot eyes and thick arms covered with gruesome tattoos staggered to their table. "Are you the girls who want to know about my boat?"

Enid flashed Elizabeth a look of alarm. "No," Elizabeth answered in a polite but business-like tone. "You must have us confused with somebody else."

He opened his eyes wider and leaned forward, bracing his elbow on their table. "My boat is for sale because I'm building a bigger one."

Elizabeth gasped as she got a whiff of his breath. A woman wearing a red leather halter top, with a rose tattooed on her chin and whose head was completely shaved, stood up at the other end of the diner and yelled, "Get back here, Peter!"

"I think someone is calling you," Elizabeth said. She struggled to appear calm, as if she were facing a vicious-looking dog.

The man smiled, showing off a row of brownish teeth. "I know. Ella is my lady but you two beautiful little things are so sweet, it breaks my heart."

The bald woman screamed, "Get back here or I'll carve my initials on your forehead."

He finally staggered back where he'd come from. Enid exhaled with a sigh of relief. "Peter the boat builder, huh? One thing we have to say about old Rosie, she sure knows where to find the liveliest nightlife."

"Come on, give the girl a break," Elizabeth said. "This place is very tame during the day. It is possible she's never been here at night."

"She sure has a loyal champion in you," Enid said.

"You'd like her too, I'm sure. Rosie is a very interesting person," Elizabeth said. "I don't think Marla and Caitlin have given her a fair chance."

"Oh yeah? What makes Rosie Shaw such an interesting person?" Enid ducked her head sheepishly. "Ooops, I'd better not mention her name too loudly in here. These might be her friends."

Elizabeth scowled at her. "Very funny, but I seriously doubt it. I think Rosie hides behind that tough exterior because she's shy."

"That's a word I'd never use to describe the Rosie I met."

"She is, and very sensitive, too. Marla rejected a story she wrote for the *Palisades Pentagon* and it nearly crushed her. I've invited her to write for us at *The Oracle*."

Enid frowned. "Why did Marla do that?"

"Rosie thinks it's because the story wasn't very good," Elizabeth replied. "Marla told her to stick to surfing."

A haggard-looking waitress approached their booth. "What do yous want?" she asked, punctuating the question with a snap of her chewing gum.

Enid and Elizabeth looked at each other. "Coffee," Enid said. "Two cups, please."

The waitress tipped her head and fluttered her eyelashes, as if a great burden had been placed on her shoulders. "The coffee ain't made."

Elizabeth smiled. "There's no hurry. Take your time."

"All right, girls, but I'm telling you, it ain't made yet."

"We understand," Enid said.

When she left, Elizabeth and Enid looked at each other and burst out laughing. "This place is a zoo," Elizabeth declared. "I'm sure Rosie had no idea the Silverhead Diner turns into a madhouse at night."

"I find it hard to believe that Marla would say something so mean to Rosie, or to anyone for that matter," Enid said, jumping right in where they'd left off.

"Me, too," Elizabeth said. "But Marla has made no secret of how much she dislikes her. One thing this whole rivalry mess has shown me is that people don't always act the way you expect. Who would have ever thought Todd could be so violent?"

Enid shook her head. "I know what you mean, Liz. Still, I just don't trust Rosie. I've learned the hard way that some people just don't deserve to be trusted."

"You're talking about your experience at Paradise Spa, aren't you?" Elizabeth guessed. Enid had accompanied the twins, their mother, Lila, and her mother to an ill-fated stay at a luxury health spa. The owner was a woman who hated Mrs. Wakefield and had been carrying a vendetta against her for decades. She'd also managed to isolate Enid from the group and nearly convinced her to stay on as an emotionally dependant slave.

"That's right," Enid said with a wry expression. "Good old Mrs. Mueller pulled me into her web of deceit and every instinctive defense I had just melted away."

Elizabeth caught her lip between her teeth, remembering how close she'd come to losing her best friend—and her mother—to that mad woman.

"Tatiana Mueller was a monster. You can't compare her to Rosie Shaw."

"I don't know about that," Enid said.

"You will after tonight."

"Whatever you say, Liz." Enid pulled out a copy of the *Palisades Pentagon* from her bag. "I just wish she'd get here."

"Me, too." Elizabeth checked her watch. Rosie was fifteen minutes late. "She might have gotten caught in some heavy traffic."

"I hope that's all it is," Enid said.

Elizabeth tapped her foot impatiently. "Me, too."

"Why don't you try calling her?" Enid suggested.

"Good idea." Elizabeth slid out of the booth and stopped. To get to the hallway where the pay phone was located, Elizabeth would have to walk the length of the dining room through the wild biker party. She grimaced over her shoulder at Enid. "If I'm not back in five minutes, come looking for me."

Enid looked up from her reading and gave Elizabeth a thumbs-up sign.

Rosie's line was busy. Frustrated, Elizabeth returned to the booth. Two steaming cups of coffee were on the table.

"Well?" Enid asked.

"Busy. I'll try back in a few minutes if she doesn't get here before that." Elizabeth picked up one of the cups, wrapping her hands around it to warm them as she took a sip.

The *Palisades Pentagon* was spread across Enid's side of the table. "These articles about Sweet Valley High are great," Enid said. "Did you get a chance to read them?"

Elizabeth peered over the rim of her cup. "Most of them."

"I love the one they wrote about *The Oracle*," Enid said. "They said such nice things about everyone on the staff."

"I didn't see that," Elizabeth said, glancing over at the paper.

"Here," Enid said, turning it around so that it was right side up from Elizabeth's angle. There was a group picture of *The Oracle* staff and a brief write-up on each member, which included biographical information, hobbies, interests, and career aspirations. Elizabeth scanned the article, too preoccupied and nervous to pay much attention.

"It must be quite an ego boost to read all those flattering things about yourself," Enid said.

Elizabeth looked at her with a blank expression. "What do you mean?"

"The article you just read." Enid took the paper back and scanned the text. "Here it is. 'Elizabeth Wakefield—a girl with beauty, brains, and a heart as big as the Pacific Ocean.' Doesn't that make you feel just the slightest bit proud?"

"Let me see that." A frightening thought occurred to Elizabeth. She grabbed the paper and urgently skimmed the page. "It says that I aspire to become a professional writer someday, and that I enjoy old movies and . . . poetry." She looked up, her body trembling in shock and horror.

Enid frowned. "What's the matter?"

"It says that my favorite poet is Christina Rossetti."

"So? She is," Enid said. "What's wrong, Elizabeth? Your face just turned chalky white. Are you sick?"

Elizabeth covered her eyes with her hand and slumped back in her seat. "I think I've made a big mistake."

"About what?"

"Wait here," Elizabeth said, sliding out of the booth. "I have to make a phone call."

"What is going on?" Enid demanded in alarm.

"I don't know yet. But stay right here and keep watch in case Rosie shows up."

Elizabeth rushed back to the phone, oblivious to the leering and catcalls coming at her from the crowd. As she dialed Marla's number, her hands shook. Marla answered on the first ring.

"What did you tell Rosie Shaw when you rejected her article for the *Pentagon*?" Elizabeth demanded without preamble.

"Elizabeth, is that you?"

"It's important, Marla. Rosie said you told her—"

"Wait a minute. I don't know what you're talking about," Marla interrupted.

"Do you remember the article she wrote about her grandmother?" Elizabeth asked urgently.

There was a pause. Then Marla said, "Rosie Shaw never wrote an article for the *Pentagon*."

Elizabeth gasped. "She never . . .?"

"No," Marla said. "And if she had, I wouldn't have rejected it. I've never rejected anything from a student—at worst, I make them revise endlessly."

A cold chill gripped Elizabeth's throat. "I have to go, Marla."

"Wait! What's this all about?" Marla demanded. "What's happening?"

"I can't talk now." Elizabeth disconnected the call, regretting her rudeness, but feeling too worried to avoid it. "Don't panic yet," she whispered to herself. She dialed Rosie's number next, and waited. *So maybe Rosie did lie and manipulate me to win my trust,* Elizabeth mused. Ending the SVH-PH War required desperate measures. Elizabeth could even understand why Rosie had done it.

Finally, a young girl answered the phone. "My sister isn't home," she said. "She went out with her boyfriend."

Elizabeth caught her bottom lip between her

teeth. "Do you happen to know where they went?"

The girl giggled. "I don't know, but Rosie said she's going to kick some Sweet Valley butt."

Elizabeth slammed down the receiver and shuddered. She'd been tricked! Rosie obviously never had any intention of showing up. Elizabeth leaned her forehead against the rough surface of the wall and moaned. She felt like such a fool. It was so clear now—Rosie had completely manipulated her, but not for the purpose of ending the feud between SVH and PH.

Elizabeth's eyes flew open as an alarming thought occurred to her. *The guys!* Rosie knew they were meeting at Bruce's house. *What have I done?*

"Hey honey, other people are waiting for the phone," a gruff voice behind her said.

Ignoring it, and the greasy man it belonged to, Elizabeth slipped another coin into the slot.

"What is she doing, making another call!" Someone shoved her from behind.

Elizabeth whirled around, her panic turning to fury. "Leave me alone!"

The guys stared at her for a moment, then walked away, grumbling. She turned back to the phone and, her hands shaking, she called Jessica.

Chapter 8

Jessica exploded. "Rosie Shaw! Liz, what are you saying? You were supposed to meet *Rosie Shaw*?"

"Yes,"—Elizabeth choked back a sob—"at a diner in Palisades. That's where I'm calling from."

"*What* is going on?"

Elizabeth groped through her pockets for a tissue. "Rosie read the article in the *Palisades Pentagon* and spoon-fed every line back to me, and I fell for it." She sniffed. "How could I be so stupid? I'll bet she's never even read Christina Rossetti."

"Get a grip! I still don't understand a word you're saying. Why were you meeting that vile creature in the first place?" Jessica asked.

Elizabeth took a deep breath. "We had worked out a plan to get the guys to stop fighting. She and I were going to meet here and then go together to talk to the guys and tell each side that the other wanted peace. It was all Rosie's idea. She said she wanted the war to end as much as I did and I believed her." Elizabeth's voice started to quiver. "But she's not here and I told her the Sweet Valley High guys were planning to meet at Bruce's house tonight."

"Oh, no. How could you do that!" Jessica screamed. "Don't you see, you've set them up?"

"I know," Elizabeth whispered.

There was a long pause on the line. Then Jessica asked, in a sharp, tense voice, "Please tell me that you didn't say anything to Rosie Shaw about me and Christian."

"I trusted her, Jessica."

"Tell me, Elizabeth!"

"I'm so sorry," Elizabeth said, sobbing.

Jessica screamed hysterically. "Something terrible is about to happen, I just know it. Christian wouldn't tell me where he was going, but I'm sure it has something to do with all this. He could get hurt. I have to go find him. Oh no, you have the Jeep, don't you? Come home right now and pick me up, Elizabeth. Then we'll head over to Bruce's."

"I'm leaving right now," Elizabeth said.

"Hurry!"

Elizabeth hung up and, ignoring the dirty looks from the people lined up to use the phone, rushed back to Enid. "Come on, we have to go," Elizabeth said.

Enid began gathering her things together. "Something's wrong, isn't it?" She looked up at Elizabeth and frowned. "You've been crying?"

Elizabeth nodded, her eyes watering all over again. "You were right about Rosie. This whole thing was a setup to trap the guys."

"Come on," Enid said. She pulled a five-dollar bill out of her bag and used it to flag down the waitress.

Elizabeth's hands were shaking as she unlocked the doors of the Jeep. "How could I have been so dumb?"

"You always assume the best about people," Enid said. "There's nothing wrong with that."

"Except when they don't deserve it." Elizabeth started the engine and peeled out of the parking lot in a flurry of kicked-up gravel. "I have a sinking feeling in my stomach that the Sweet Valley High guys are about to be ambushed," she said as she raced down the winding road. "And it's all my fault!"

"The element of surprise will be key," Bruce announced as he leaned over the pool table for a shot.

They'd been hanging out in the Patmans' rec room for hours, hatching plot after plot to get back at the PH guys for kidnapping Winston. Todd

132

looked at the other SVH guys, trying to gauge their reactions to Bruce's harebrained idea, the most bizarre one yet—a car jacking.

Todd shook his head, amazed. He still hadn't found the right moment to make his speech, but given the rapt expressions he saw on the guys' faces, he doubted anyone would listen.

"Ken and I will hide in the back of McMullen's Range Rover and wait," Bruce continued. "When he arrives and gets in, we'll grab him. Then we'll signal for the rest of you guys. Ronnie, Kirk, and Aaron will come with us in McMullen's car. Blubber, Tim, Danny, and the rest of you will go with Todd. We'll probably need a few more drivers."

"Where do we take McMullen?" Danny asked.

"Seems like a lot of trouble," Kirk said. "Why don't we just dump him out along the way and take the car?"

Bruce raised his hand and gestured for silence. "Hold on and let me finish. You're going to love this." A wicked gleam twinkled in his eyes. "We'll all drive over to Big Mesa, leave old Greg at the town dock and push his car off the pier. Then—as we watch it sink to the bottom of the ocean—we will *party*."

"So big deal, we leave him on the dock," Aaron said. "All he has to do is walk to a phone and call somebody to come get him." Several of the guys nodded, grumbling.

Bruce scowled at them. "*Leaving* him there, that was just an expression. What I mean is we'll tie him to the dock. Greg McMullen isn't going to go anywhere until morning." He turned to Todd and grinned. "Your shot."

Todd blinked, nonplussed.

Bruce grinned. "Pool, remember?"

Todd picked up the cue stick he'd left on the rail of the pool table and gazed at the configuration of balls on the green baize.

"Solids," Bruce said.

Todd looked up, annoyed. "I knew that."

"I was just trying to help."

The room fell silent while Todd took his turn— and missed by several feet. Bruce raised his eyebrows but said nothing as he rubbed chalk on the end of his cue stick and resumed his position at the table.

"When is this diabolical deed supposed to take place?" Winston asked. It was the first time he'd spoken all night, Todd realized.

Bruce slowly circled the table, as if he were stalking the game. "On Thursday," he said. "The night before the Palisades-Big Mesa game."

"Is that why we're taking him to Big Mesa?" Blubber asked.

Bruce pointed his finger like a gun at him and smiled. "Give that big boy a prize."

Danny frowned. "I'm not sure I understand the connection."

Bruce pulled his arm back and aimed his shot. "Okay, let me explain it for the not-so-bright among us. A dirty team like the Palisades Pumas is going to make enemies all over the place, right? So it's logical to assume that the Big Mesa football team hates the Pumas as much as we do."

Kirk slapped his fist against his other hand. "Brilliant, my man! And if we wear disguises and gloves, who can prove it wasn't the Big Mesa guys pulling the job to cripple the Pumas' chances of winning the next day?"

"Not only that," Bruce said, "but I have it from a very reliable source that several scouts from big-name universities will be at that game. Greg McMullen isn't the only player up for an athletic scholarship, but with him out of the picture, the whole team is going to look bad."

"What about the Big Mesa players?" Winston said.

Bruce pinned him with a level stare. "Are you wimping out on us?"

Winston gulped. "No, um . . . I was just wondering if it was fair to, you know, let them take the blame for what we're doing."

Bruce shrugged. "Hey, with McMullen off the field and the Pumas floundering, Big Mesa is going to look pretty darn hot. We're doing those guys a big favor."

"Oh," Winston mumbled. "I get it." Todd could tell that he didn't.

"That'll teach those PH pigs not to mess with us," Ken declared. The guys seemed to be in complete agreement as they raised their voices in a chorus of macho cheers and threats: "We'll have them wishing they'd never started this war."

"They're going to be sorry they ever heard of Sweet Valley High."

"Gladiators rule!"

"Death to the Pumas!"

Bruce slapped Winston's back. "We're going to make those guys pay for what they did to you."

Todd watched them, shaking his head. Guys who were supposed to have brains in their heads were chanting the most stupid things he'd ever heard and strutting about without a clue. They reminded him of the roosters he'd seen at a farm he once visited when he was little. "Wait a minute," he said, raising his hands for attention. "Look at yourselves. Look at what all of this fighting has reduced us to. We're talking about car jacking! I still can't believe I actually went to court. And now I'm planning something that will probably land me in jail—that's no way to live." He looked around the room and felt a glimmer of hope. The guys were actually listening and nodding their heads. Todd turned to Bruce. His expression had softened a bit—although he was still maintaining his tough exterior.

Holding on to his advantage, Todd continued. "I think it's time for us to get real," he said. "This war is going nowhere; surely all of you can see that too. If we would all just—"

Ken jumped to his feet. "What was that noise?"

Todd held his breath, suddenly alert. Then he heard it—a racket of whooping and yelling coming from outside. "What the—" he began, bounding up the stairs with the rest of the Sweet Valley High guys at his heels.

They didn't see anyone outside, but the sounds grew louder. The immediate area was illuminated by flood lamps, although shadowy trees and hedges could easy hide plenty of danger. Todd had a sinking feeling that his premonition of disaster was about to come true.

"Who's out there?" Bruce called.

No one answered.

"Quit hiding," he ordered. "Or are you just too wimpy to face us?"

The noise lessened. Todd held his breath, waiting for something to happen. He could almost hear the pounding of his heart. Then Rosie Shaw stepped out from behind a tree.

"Hi, Todd," she said with a sneer. "Elizabeth told me you guys would be here."

Elizabeth. Todd felt an icy cold surge of fear squeezing his throat. *What if they've kidnapped her?* he thought, overcome with dread. What had they done to her to make her talk? If they hurt her, so much as laid a hand on her, he'd . . . He clenched his hands into two rock-hard fists and roared, "Where is she? What have you done with Elizabeth?"

Whistles, kissing noises, and hoots of laughter rang out from the shadows, mocking him. Rosie shook her head, pretending regret. "The poor girl is probably still sitting in the Silverhead Diner in Palisades, waiting for me. Dizzy Lizzy and I are best friends now, haven't you heard? We were supposed to get together tonight and spread the message of peace and goodwill to all you mean old guys." Rosie laughed, a shrill witch's cackle. "Oh, Todd." She shook her head and sighed dramatically. "Did anyone ever tell you that you've got the dumbest girlfriend in the universe?"

As the meaning of her words sunk in, Todd felt a blood-chilling anger growing deep inside of him—big enough to include Elizabeth. Again she'd brought him immeasurable grief by failing to support him. She'd actually betrayed him and all the SVH guys. The realization hit him like a sledgehammer across the face.

"But then again, maybe Elizabeth isn't as innocent as she seems," Rosie taunted. "Who knows? She could have planned this whole thing to help us destroy you because she likes Palisades guys better—just like her sister."

Todd lurched forward, then stopped himself. No matter what buttons Rosie Shaw pushed, he was determined to control his rage. Maybe he could even think of something to say which would end this ordeal.

Just then a shattering cry rang out and the Palisades High guys came running from the shadows. Their faces were streaked with brightly colored war paint in grotesque designs. Whooping and yelling, they ran around the Patman estate.

"Come on, let's get them," Kirk said.

Bruce shook his head, his gaze scanning the area. "No," he said. "We'll let them come to us, and tire themselves out while they're at it."

The SVH guys waited in tense stillness, exchanging wary glances. A strong breeze whistled through the tree branches and a small animal scurried across the yard. Todd's stomach churned with anticipation and dread.

"Gee whiz," Winston said, "those guys look so pretty with their faces painted. Why didn't we think of wearing makeup?" No one smiled. Winston ducked his head sheepishly. "Sorry, just trying to entertain the troops."

Bruce glared at him. "Just stay in back and keep quiet. And try not to get punched in the nose again."

Finally the war cries began sounding closer, signaling the end of the Palisades war dance. The SVH guys spread out in a line across the back lawn and prepared to confront their enemies. The two groups faced each other across a span of several yards. The PH guys looked hideous and evil under the unnatural glow of the outdoor lighting. No one moved. They seemed to be playing a deadly waiting game. Everyone's nerves stretched to the limit, they watched each other to see who would take the first step. Todd had lost all hope of being able to bring any shred of common sense to this mess.

A lethal force was about to explode. Todd's heart squeezed shut. He knew with gut-certainty that within the next few heartbeats, someone would strike the deadly spark.

They had reached the point of no return.

Wondering what the Palisades guys were thinking, he glanced across the dividing space. Greg McMullen was staring at him, flashing a malevolent smile. Something bright caught Todd's attention. With an overwhelming feeling of trepidation, he lowered his gaze and saw a pair of brass knuckles glinting on Greg McMullen's hand.

Chapter 9

Calico Drive was quiet at that time of night and the air was cool and damp. Jessica stood in the front doorway of her house, watching for Elizabeth. She jumped as the phone rang, her nerves already strained to the breaking point. She desperately hoped that it was Christian calling to tell her everything was fine. But as she waited for the answering machine to pick up the call, a whisper of cold dread seized her by the throat, making it impossible to breathe.

"Hello, Elizabeth. It's Marla. Please call me. I have to know what's going on. Caitlin is at my house. Call as soon as you get home, no matter how late. Please!"

Jessica closed her eyes and exhaled the breath she'd been holding. She'd lost count of how many times Marla Daniels had called in the last few minutes, her voice sounding increasingly hysterical with each one—and each one pushing Jessica a little closer to losing her mind.

A car turned the corner, its headlights coming straight for her. Jessica's stomach lurched in expectation as she got ready to pounce on it. But as the car came closer, and pulled into the driveway next door, she realized it was Mrs. Beckwith, the neighbor, in her yellow Buick.

Jessica shrieked in frustration. She really was losing touch with reality. If Elizabeth didn't hurry up and get home, Jessica was sure she'd go completely insane.

She tried to block the frightening scenarios her imagination insisted on creating, but they pushed their way through her mind like termites in a wooden shack, replaying the climax of every suspenseful movie she'd ever seen, with Christian starring as the tragic hero.

What if the Palisades guys had gotten hold of guns and went looking for a shoot-out at Bruce's house and Christian got killed in the cross fire? What if they concocted a bomb and Christian tried to defuse it and cut the wrong wire and was blown up into a million pieces? What if they captured one of the Sweet Valley guys and Christian offered to die in his place? What if, besides sticking a notice under his windshield wiper, they'd also booby-trapped his car, cutting the brake line or something? What if they . . .

Finally, Elizabeth arrived. With a whoop of relief, Jessica slammed the front door shut and ran to the curb. There was nothing more frustrating than waiting around paralyzed in the face of danger. When she hopped into the front seat of the Jeep, she felt her adrenaline kick in. She was ready to do whatever it took to help Christian, even if she had to take on all the guys single-handedly.

But instead of putting the Jeep in gear and peeling out of there, Elizabeth turned to Jessica and enveloped her in a big sisterly hug. Enid, who was sitting in the backseat, looked on sorrowfully. When her eyes met Jessica's, Enid mouthed the words, "She's really upset."

Jessica's feeling of urgency was way past the tolerance level, but she forced herself to remain civil and return her sister's hug. "It's okay, Elizabeth," she said, trying to sound reassuring, though her voice was edged with desperation. "You made a mistake. Now we have to hurry up and get to Bruce's house."

Elizabeth backed away, swiped at her damp cheeks with her wrist, and turned to the task of driving. "I still can't figure out how I could have been so stupid! You'd think I would've gotten suspicious when Rosie started asking me about the security at the Patman Mansion." She began sobbing again and nearly missed the turn off Calico Drive. Enid and Jessica both shouted at the same time. Elizabeth swerved, taking the corner a bit too sharply. The Jeep hopped the curb onto their neighbor's front yard, knocked out an obnoxious lawn ornament and ran over a clump of pansies.

Jessica glared at Elizabeth. "Are you okay to drive?" Elizabeth nodded, her eyes staring straight ahead.

"I never liked that stupid thing anyway," Enid said. "Why would anyone put a plastic lady bending over with her underwear showing on their front lawn?"

"It's just that she sounded so sincere," Elizabeth said. "But still, I shouldn't have been so quick to trust Rosie."

"Don't beat yourself up about it," Enid said, patting Elizabeth's shoulder.

Jessica remained quiet. Once again, her frustration level shot up higher. The drive seemed to be taking forever and her gut was screaming: *disaster, disaster, disaster!* What if the Palisades guys had done something horrible and lured Christian into it in order to frame him? With his reputation, who would believe in his innocence? They might have planted so much evidence that even a high-priced, fancy lawyer couldn't save him. What if he was forced to plea bargain, and had to spend years in prison for a crime he didn't commit?

"If anything happens to the guys, it'll be all my fault," Elizabeth was wailing. "I'm scared to death of what we might find when we get to Bruce's house. What if they get into another huge fight like they did last week?"

Jessica couldn't take any more. Her feeling of panic was reaching a dangerous level, so huge and powerful she was afraid it would blow out her teeth. She turned to Elizabeth and shouted, "Shut up! I've already dreamed up a million horrible scenarios on my own, thank you very much. I don't need to hear yours as well."

Elizabeth gave her a sideways glance and mumbled, "Sorry."

"You're forgiven, all right? No more 'I'm so sorry's. Just pay attention to the road and drive faster!"

Elizabeth sniffed and nodded. No one in the Jeep said another word as they made their way across town to Sweet Valley's ritzy hill section.

Jessica closed her eyes. *Christian!* she screamed silently, the name echoing in her head.

"We heard you guys asking if we were wimps," Greg McMullen said with a sickening, oily tone in his voice. "The Pumas never walk away from a challenge. Do we, guys?" All the PH guys shook their heads and muttered their agreement.

Sitting on the other side of the yard, Rosie

Shaw piped up. "Excuse me? Let's not forget the dangerous Palisades ladies, darling."

Todd shook his head in disgust. She'd made herself right at home, stretched out on one of the Patmans' decorative wrought iron lawn chairs.

McMullen glanced at her, a slight narrowing of his eyes signaling his irritation. "As I was saying. Me and my friends have talked things over and we decided Sweet Valley needs to be taught a few lessons. It's nothing personal—we figure this whole town is stupid and it just happened to rub off on you."

"We'll see who teaches who a lesson," Bruce shot back. "Because if anybody comes from a town of idiots, it's you guys."

"Palisades stinks, too," Kirk added.

Greg sneered at him. "Why don't you come over and say that to my face, boy."

Just then, a blue Volkswagen bus came careening up the Patmans' driveway. Everyone turned to look. Todd saw all of Ken's muscles tighten up, his hands clenched into fists. Christian Gorman jumped out of the van and rushed to the middle of the group.

Ken stepped forward, his chin thrust upwards. "Over here, slime bag," he called out, raising his fists. "Come on, Gorman, you and me, right now."

Christian turned to him. "I'm not here to fight with you, man." Todd caught a glimpse of something in his expression, sadness, or regret, maybe even guilt—but he doubted Ken would pick up on it, furious as he was.

"Then what are you here for?" Greg McMullen challenged.

Christian turned to the line of PH guys, his lips twisting into a crooked smile. However, his eyes remained hard as steel. "Nice touch, the war paint." His gaze moved from face to face. "But to answer your question, I'm here because I got your message. At least I assume it's from you guys. There's no signature on it." He pulled a folded sheet of lined notepaper from the back pocket of his jeans, opened it and tossed it on the ground at his feet. Then he planted his foot on the paper, grinding it into the dirt with the heel of his boot. "I wonder which one of my good friends here stuck this gracious invitation on the windshield of my van. It said if I didn't show up here tonight, I could 'kiss the cheerleader goodbye forever.'" He looked up, his eyes filled with rage. "So what's that supposed to mean, huh? Are you guys ready to start executing each other's girlfriends?"

Greg McMullen stepped forward, pointing an accusing finger at Christian's face. "You shouldn't have messed around with her in the first place. Palisades is where you're from and don't forget it."

Christian's eyes narrowed. "McMullen, I've saved your neck more times than I can count. I

147

don't have to take this from you. Especially since you don't have a clue about Jessica and me."

"And you don't have a clue about being loyal," someone shouted. Todd turned to the speaker, a PH guy whose face was streaked with green and black paint.

"Doug's right," another PH guy agreed. "Going out with a Sweet Valley girl tells everyone in Palisades that you're turning your back on us."

The guy standing next to him waved his fists. "We've stuck by you for a long time, Christian, and now you're treating us like dirt."

Bruce snorted. "That's because you *are* dirt. You're all dirty scum as far as I can see." He turned to Christian. "And you!" Bruce spit on the ground dramatically. "You should've stayed on your own turf. We don't want you and your kind hanging around our girls."

"Yeah," Kirk said. "It's not our fault that your Palisades girls are all dogs!"

Rosie stood up and yelled, "I'm going to kill you, jerk!"

Christian raised his hands, pleading. "Listen to me, everyone. We have to get something straight, right here and now. I'm not with Jessica to make some kind of statement to anyone. The fact that she's from Sweet Valley means nothing to me. I didn't even know where she lived when I first met her. She and I have a good thing going. Sweet Valley and Palisades have nothing to do with it. This is our own business—Jessica's and mine." His voice became softer and trembled with emotion. "We love each other and no one will ever change that."

"I don't think so, Gorman," Ken said, his face distorted with anger. "We're going to fight this out to the end and when it's over, we'll see who's left standing."

"It sure ain't going to be you, windbag," Greg McMullen taunted. A few PH guys chuckled in response.

"You guys are acting like mindless idiots," Christian said. "The fighting has to stop! Can't you get it through your thick heads?"

"Yeah, right," the guy standing next to Greg said. "You're so hot to sell us out now that you're kissing up to the enemy."

"Yeah," another said. "Are you trying to earn points with your little SVH cheerleader?"

Christian groaned in frustration. "Why is it so hard for you guys to understand that Jessica and I love each other? I'm telling you, this is the real thing."

No one seemed interested. Todd listened as accusations continued to fly back and forth, raising the tension level higher and higher. In a far corner of his mind, it occurred to him how ironic it was that the guys of SVH and PH had finally found something to agree on: The Christian Gorman-

Jessica Wakefield match should never have happened.

Jessica's heart was racing as they drove up the hill to the Patman Mansion. "Come on, Liz. Step on it!"

"I've got it to the metal, Jess. Hold on." She pulled into the Patmans' driveway and jerked to a stop.

"Oh, look, there they are," Enid said, pointing to the area near the back of the house.

The guys were standing in a huddle with Christian in the middle. Jessica covered her lips with her hand, stifling a cry of relief. He looked so vulnerable standing there alone, surrounded by the others. Her heart went out to him. But at least he was all right.

"I see Christian," Elizabeth said. "But where's Todd?"

"He's standing near the juniper bushes," Enid said, indicating the dark greenery that flanked both sides of the back entrance.

"Oh yes, I see him." Elizabeth slumped back in the car seat and exhaled a long, shaky breath. "I was so scared we'd find a disaster here, but it looks like they're finally talking to each other."

"Guess the guys are smarter than we thought," Enid said with a wry smile.

Jessica sniffed. "Yeah. Maybe they've decided

to grow up at last." She popped open the glove box and rummaged through the contents for any make-up odds and ends she could find. Her face probably looked frightful by now and she'd left the house without her bag. "I just want to go get Christian out of there and leave. This whole situation has been one big nightmare and I'm sick of—"

Suddenly Elizabeth and Enid screamed.

"What—" Jessica looked up and gasped in horror. A huge fight had broken out, as instantaneous as a flash of lightning and worse than anything she'd imagined. The lust for blood seemed to rage at fever pitch. Bodies were crashing against each other, toppling over, piling on top of the unfortunate ones who fell. The noise alone was terrifying, a spine-chilling combination of angry shouting, the thud of fists smacking into flesh, and deep moans of pain.

Todd was holding someone by the collar, punching his face over and over, until Doug Riker kicked Todd flat-footed in the back, knocking him into a tree trunk. Danny Porter, his face coated with blood, was locked in a wrestling match with someone. Doug Brewster, from Palisades, rammed into them headfirst.

Glass shattered as an errant rock missed its intended target and flew through a lower window. A PH guy held Kirk Anderson down while another kicked him viciously in the stomach. Christian tried to break up two guys who had their hands around each other's throat, only to be attacked by both of them in return.

Jessica screamed and screamed, but her voice sounded as if it were far away. She felt split in two—one part of her was writhing in anguish, taking in the horror as it unfolded, while another side of her seemed to be floating high above the scene, watching everything in a state of numb shock.

She watched as Todd staggered across the yard and fell against a PH guy, sending them both crashing to the ground. Three other guys jumped on top of them, turning it into a heap of thrashing limbs. She was vaguely aware of Elizabeth squeezing her hand.

Jessica caught sight of Rosie Shaw sitting on the sidelines, her expression as cool as can be. *She's actually enjoying this,* Jessica realized. Her blood began to boil. It dawned on Jessica that Rosie had played a pivotal role in orchestrating this whole nightmare.

The fight moved toward the Patmans' huge pool, where the light was dim and shadowy. Three of the PH guys grabbed Kirk Anderson and tried to push him into the pool, but Christian moved in and knocked them off of him. Then Ken shouted something at Christian and started running toward him, but Greg McMullen intercepted him. A cold, hard fist of fear squeezed Jessica's stomach as she watched Greg jump onto Ken's back, grab a fistful of his blond hair and bang his head against the ground.

"He's going to smash Ken's skull!" she heard herself scream.

Suddenly Christian threw himself on top of Greg and dragged him off of Ken. Greg twisted to get free of Christian's hold, striking out with his fists and trying to kick at Christian's legs.

Jessica yelled, "Christian, look out!" as a PH guy ran over and blindsided him, knocking him off Greg.

Christian staggered toward the pool, his arms groping as he tried to regain his balance. Jessica's scream froze in her throat. In nightmarish slow motion, Christian collapsed, hitting his head on the pavement with a loud thud, and fell into the deep end of the pool.

Chapter 10

Elizabeth screamed, but Jessica held her breath as she watched the shimmering blue water for the slightest movement, any sign which would indicate Christian was all right. She felt paralyzed, afraid to move, as if by remaining still as stone she could affect Christian's safety.

Enid shook Jessica's and Elizabeth's shoulders. "Come on! We have to do something. The guys don't see him," Enid shouted, breaking through Jessica's stupor. Elizabeth stopped screaming and all three girls jumped out of the Jeep.

Jessica sprang into action. Without a second thought, she ran as fast as she could to the edge of the pool and dived in, shoes and all. With powerful strokes fueled by sheer desperation, she swam to the dark figure lying motionless on the bottom of the pool.

She clutched at his shoulders, as if to shake him. His stillness frightened her, but she pushed all her fears and doubts aside and forced herself to think only positive thoughts. *He is going to make it,* she vowed.

Christian was lying on his side. Jessica maneuvered herself behind him and wrapped her left arm across his chest. She pulled him away from the bottom of the pool. Kicking her legs hard enough to feel her muscles burn, she struggled to the surface. Her lungs felt as if they were on fire and ready to burst. A familiar dizzy sensation began to invade her state of alertness, shooting off an alarm in her mind. She was running out of oxygen.

Jessica debated whether to let go of Christian and shoot up to the surface for a gulp of air. But she realized, even if it meant she'd drown, she would never release her hold on him. They'd surface together or not at all.

Help me, Christian, she silently pleaded as she fought against losing consciousness herself. Her legs and arms felt as if they were about to give out and a twinge of hopelessness began to invade her frantic struggling.

Suddenly a surge of determination filled her. An almost magical second wind kicked in, giving her a boost of power as Jessica found the strength to keep pushing for the surface.

As soon as her face was out of the water, Jessica gasped for air, hungrily filling her lungs. She hauled Christian to the side of the pool and held him there, braced against the pool wall with his head above water. She breathed in and out in deep gulps, her body limp with exhaustion.

Elizabeth and Enid were there waiting. They pulled Christian, while she pushed, and together the girls managed to drag him out of the pool as the guys continued to smash fists and knock each other to the ground. Elizabeth pushed on Christian's back a few times, then rolled him over, faceup as Jessica hoisted herself over the edge. She crawled on her knees over to him and gazed at the face she'd grown to love with all her heart.

His lips were purple and swollen and there was a grayish pallor to his skin. "Somebody call nine-one-one!" she screamed.

Elizabeth was kneeling on the other side of Christian. She reached over and squeezed Jessica's shoulder reassuringly. "Enid just went inside to call them," she said.

The guys seemed to realize finally that something had happened and suddenly the fighting stopped. Everyone rushed over and huddled around Christian's still body.

"Is he all right?" someone asked.

"Is he breathing?"

"He's not moving."

"What happened?"

Elizabeth placed her hand on Christian's forehead and gently pushed his head down at an angle, raising his chin. She looked up and said, "Jessica! CPR until they get here."

Reacting to the direct command in her sister's tone, Jessica snapped to attention. She positioned her hands, one on top of the other, on Christian's chest and watched as Elizabeth inhaled deeply, lowered her head to his and forced her breath into his lungs. His chest rose with a hollow sounding whoosh. After two breaths, Jessica began to administer heart massage.

Jessica focused all the emotional energy swirling inside her into saving Christian as she and Elizabeth worked in harmony. The guys, the fight, Rosie, the past, and the future all faded away. The only element left of reality for Jessica was the CPR rhythm—breathe in, breathe out, and push one, two, three, four, five. . . .

They continued for what seemed like forever, but nothing was happening. An edgy feeling of panic came over Jessica. "Please, Christian!" she begged as she pushed on his chest, willing his heart to spring to life. But Christian remained unconscious.

Jessica refused to believe what the logical side

of her mind was telling her. "No, I won't let you go," she cried. "Do you hear me, Christian! I need you. You promised me things . . . the sand castle, remember?" She choked back a sob. "You know I have ways of making you remember."

She swiped at her eyes and waited as Elizabeth breathed into Christian's mouth. Then Jessica administered another series of chest massages. "He's going to make it," she announced defiantly, daring anyone to contradict her. "He is. I'm sure of it." Jessica looked up at her sister. Elizabeth's face was wet with tears.

Moments later, Elizabeth heard the ambulance coming, the keening wail of its siren growing louder and louder until it finally reached the Patman Mansion and pulled into the driveway. Its flashing lights cut through the night's darkness, illuminating the surrounding horror with a pulsing reddish glow.

Two paramedics rushed over to Christian's side. Elizabeth moved out of the way as one of them, a dark-haired woman with large, expressive eyes, placed a piece of equipment over Christian's nose and mouth. "This will breathe for him," she said.

Elizabeth nudged Jessica. "We have to move out of their way so they can help Christian," she whispered close to her sister's ear. Jessica didn't move. Her gaze remained fixed on Christian. Elizabeth gently tugged on her arm, pulling her a few steps back from Christian's body.

The paramedic turned and looked up at Jessica and Elizabeth. "You've both done an excellent job. If this guy pulls through, he'll have you girls to thank."

Jessica raised her chin a notch and corrected the woman. "*When* he pulls through, you mean. He *is* going to make it," she said, her voice firm and confident.

Elizabeth saw the two paramedics exchange looks of concern. The woman continued to work on Christian while the other, a man with thinning gray hair and dark eyebrows, asked questions about the accident and reported everything over his radio. Elizabeth shuddered as Christian Gorman, alive and vital only a short time ago, was now reduced to a list of statistics and medical jargon: "Male Caucasian, late teens, estimated one-hundred-seventy pounds . . . head trauma, respiratory failure, possible internal injury . . . condition unstable . . . coming in on a code blue . . ."

The paramedics continued their efforts to resuscitate Christian. Elizabeth and Jessica held on to each other for support as they and the others watched in stunned silence. A movement to her left caught Elizabeth's attention. She turned and saw Ken stepping forward from the group to stand on the other side of Jessica. His expression was pained, with a bleary look of despair in his eyes.

Elizabeth felt a warm hand clasp hers. She turned to see Todd standing next to her. Their eyes met. His were filled with compassion and remorse. Tears rolled down her cheeks as she squeezed his hand, silently thanking him for coming to her side.

After working on Christian for a few brief moments, the paramedics rolled him onto a stretcher and rushed him to the ambulance. Jessica, Elizabeth, Ken, and Todd followed, with the others close behind them. When they reached the ambulance, Jessica stood over Christian's body, clinging to Elizabeth and Ken.

"Christian! Please, Christian!" she sobbed, as her whole body trembled.

The female paramedic held Jessica back while her partner pushed the stretcher into the ambulance. Although they acted with smooth, professional efficiency, Elizabeth could see by their grave expressions that this tragedy had affected them as well. Once the stretcher was secured inside, the woman released Jessica and urged her forward. "Your turn," she said. "Hop in."

Without hesitation, Jessica leaped forward and jumped into the ambulance. Just as the female paramedic was about to shut the doors, Elizabeth leaned over and whispered softly, so Jessica wouldn't hear, "Do you think Christian will be okay?"

She turned to Elizabeth and shook her head sadly. "I'm sorry. I think we're looking at a DOA."

Elizabeth reeled back as if she'd been socked in the jaw. *Dead on arrival.* The words flashed across her mind as the piercing wail of the ambulance siren roared to life.

Todd put his arm around Elizabeth's shoulders and hugged her close to his side as they watched the ambulance drive away.

"All right, everyone," Bruce announced, taking command of the situation. "Let's go! Todd, Ken . . . who else is driving?"

Barry and Kirk waved their arms in the air. Greg McMullen also raised his hand. "My Range Rover and Doug's BMW are parked at the bottom of the hill."

Bruce nodded. "Okay then, everyone going to the hospital, find a seat."

Elizabeth seemed to be in shock as she gazed about at the sudden flurry of action. Todd clasped her hand and led her to his car, his heart aching for her. "Wait a minute," she said, stopping in her tracks. "I have my Jeep. I can't just leave it here." Her eyes watered as she looked up at him with an expression of deep despair. "Oh, Todd—I can't even think."

He wrapped his arms around her for a brief moment. "It's going to be all right," he said, trying to believe it himself. Enid and Winston were standing a few feet away. Todd waved them over.

"Elizabeth, are you okay?" Enid asked.

"I don't know," she answered.

"Would you guys follow us in the Jeep?" Todd asked.

Enid nodded. "Of course."

Elizabeth gave Enid her keys and murmured, "Thanks." Then she turned to Todd. "The paramedic said she didn't think he'd make it."

Todd opened the passenger door of his car. "What do they know?" he grumbled.

Tim Nelson, Bryce Fisherman, and two PH guys jumped into the backseat. With the car fully loaded, Todd drove to Joshua Fowler Memorial as fast as he could, chanting to himself the whole way, *Christian is going to make it . . . Christian will pull through . . .* While next to him, Elizabeth stared straight ahead, softly crying.

Todd and the rest of the caravan pulled into the parking lot in front of the emergency room. With a chorus of slamming doors, everyone jumped out and ran to the entrance.

Inside, the fluorescent lights seemed unusually bright and cast an eerie yellow shadow over everyone's face. Todd wrinkled his nose at the smell which permeated the air—a thick combination of disinfectant, rubbing alcohol, old coffee, and body odor. A nurse on duty rushed over to them, her pale eyebrows raised expectantly.

"We're here for Christian Gorman," Elizabeth said urgently.

The nurse stood before them with her arms spread out, as though she wanted to block their entering. "All of you?" she asked.

"We're his friends," someone behind Todd said.

"Okay," the nurse said, "come on in and have a seat in the waiting area, please."

"How is Christian?" Elizabeth asked.

"Yeah, can we see him?"

"Is he going to be all right?"

"Has he woken up yet?"

The nurse raised her hands, palms forward, calling for silence. "I'm sorry, there isn't any word on his condition yet. The doctors are with him now. But I promise I'll let you know as soon as possible. In the meantime, I would appreciate your patience." Then the nurse turned to Elizabeth. "I assume that was your twin sister who arrived with the ambulance?"

"Yes, Jessica. Where is she?" Elizabeth asked.

"She's around here somewhere." The nurse's eyes narrowed in a look of concern. "She's extremely upset."

"I know," Elizabeth said. "She and Christian were very close. Please tell her I'm here if you see her."

The nurse nodded. "I will."

The crowd moved into the designated waiting area, but no one bothered with the chairs. Instead they all paced nervously. Todd watched the minutes ticking by on the large wall clock over the nurses' station. He was caught in a never-ending nightmare. Every time he felt as if he were about to wake up, a slimy claw would reach out and pull him back down.

Ken walked over to him, his expression bleak. "I didn't mean it," Ken said. He jammed his hands into the front pockets of his jeans and looked into Todd's eyes. "What I said earlier, about wishing he were, you know . . . dead." His voice cracked and he took a deep breath.

Todd put his hand on his friend's shoulder. "I know you didn't. Lately we've all been saying crazy things we really didn't mean." He glanced at Elizabeth. She squeezed his hand.

"You were right," Ken said. "When you said it was time to end this stupid war, we should've listened. I can't believe how ridiculous I've been acting. Whatever happens to Gorman is all my fault."

"No it isn't," Elizabeth said. "Ken, you can't blame yourself."

"Oh, no? If he hadn't pulled McMullen off of me, he wouldn't be where he is now." A film of moisture turned Ken's blue eyes unusually bright. "It should've been me they carried in on a stretcher."

As he walked away, Todd and Elizabeth looked at each other sadly. Elizabeth glanced over his shoulder and pointed. "There's Jessica," she said.

Todd turned around and saw her. Jessica was running from doctor to doctor, desperate for information about Christian. Elizabeth called to her.

"They won't tell me anything!" Jessica said, rushing over to them. "They won't even let me see him."

Elizabeth put her arm around Jessica's shoulder, every bit the big sister, Todd thought. "They'll let us know as soon as they can," Elizabeth said in a comforting voice.

"He never regained consciousness in the ambulance, Liz. What do you think that means?" Jessica asked.

"I don't know for sure," Elizabeth said. Her eyes met Todd's and a wary looked passed between them. "Jessica, I'm sure they're doing everything they can for him," she said. "But you do understand his condition is very serious, don't you?"

"Of course I do!" Jessica snapped. "I'm not an idiot." Then, as if to soften her sharp retort, she leaned her head on Elizabeth's shoulder. "I'm so scared, Liz."

"We all are," Elizabeth whispered soothingly.

Todd saw Winston talking to Rosie Shaw. Greg McMullen was standing at the nurses' station, answering questions on Christian's personal information for their files. Someone said they'd called his parents. Time passed excruciatingly slowly.

Finally a young, lanky doctor with a curly red beard approached the group in the waiting room. He was dressed in green scrubs, with a stethoscope around his neck. "Hello, I'm Doctor Morales, Chief of Emergency Medicine."

Todd and Elizabeth glanced at each other with panic in their eyes, and Todd knew she was remembering the same thing he was—when they'd first met Dr. Morales after they'd gotten into a terrible motorcycle accident. Elizabeth had nearly died then, Todd painfully recalled. But now, by the weary slope of the doctor's shoulders as he stood there before them, Todd had the sinking feeling Christian wasn't going to be as lucky.

No one exhaled as they waited for the doctor to speak. Todd shifted uneasily. He had been as anxious as everyone else to hear about Christian's condition. But now he was suddenly gripped with the desire to send Dr. Morales away. He wasn't ready to know. He wanted to escape, to wake up from the terror. He squeezed Elizabeth's hand, grateful she was at his side, and braced himself for the inevitable.

But Todd found he wasn't prepared at all.

"I'm sorry to have to tell you this," the doctor began. "Christian Gorman has died."

As the words sunk in, Todd felt as if the earth was cracking open under his feet. The rushing of blood through his ears sounded like a speeding train. For a moment, he'd forgotten where he was. The only thing he was aware of was the dark abyss in which he was sinking.

Everyone seemed suspended in the shock of the moment. Then into the heavy silence, Jessica screamed, "No!" She sank to the floor, her body crumpled as if all her strength had drained out of her. Her wailing cries seemed to reverberate off the tiled walls. Ken stepped forward and helped Elizabeth get her into a chair.

Todd glanced around the room, seeing the remorse on everyone's face—being from Sweet Valley or Palisades no longer seemed to matter. Greg McMullen was crying openly, tears streaming down his face. Rosie Shaw was weeping on Winston's shoulder. Aaron was talking to Doug Riker, both of them shaking their heads in disbelief. The group was united in their grief.

Todd exhaled a shaky breath, a few tears rolling unchecked down his face. The sad realization occurred to him that it had taken a death to end the war.

Dr. Morales continued to describe the extent of Christian's injuries. Apparently he'd broken his neck when he fell into the pool. "I know you're all very distressed right now," the doctor added, "but Sergeant O'Riley of the SVPD would like to ask you all some questions about the events leading up to this tragedy."

When the police officer arrived, Elizabeth asked him if she could take Jessica home. "My sister isn't in any condition to speak with you right now," she said.

Sergeant O'Riley glanced at Jessica, who was sitting hunched over in a chair, sobbing into her hands. "Yes, I agree," he said. "Call the station tomorrow and set up a time to come down and give your statements."

"I'll do that," Elizabeth promised.

The first guys the sergeant wanted to question were those who had been arrested Saturday night—including Todd. Elizabeth gasped when his name was called.

Todd turned and looked deep into her eyes. "Don't worry about me, Liz. I'm going to tell them the truth. Whatever I have coming. . . ." He shrugged. "I guess it's time for me to take responsibility for my own actions."

Elizabeth sniffed and wrapped her arms around him. "I love you."

"I love you, too," he whispered.

Todd, Ken, and Enid helped Elizabeth get Jessica into the backseat of Ken's car. Elizabeth jumped in after her and Todd shut the door behind them. He stood back and watched them drive away, his hands jammed deep into the pockets of his denim jacket.

Chapter 11

Todd arrived at the Wakefields' home hours later. Although it was well past midnight, he couldn't wait until the following day to see Elizabeth. The strain of the past few weeks throbbed painfully throughout his whole body. After all that had happened, he needed to be reminded of the goodness which was still part of his life.

He walked up to the front entrance, but before he had a chance to knock, the door opened. Elizabeth stood there, looking up at him with eyes that were red and swollen. His heart ached for her and once again, he shuddered to think how close he'd come to losing her forever. A feeling of agony squeezed his throat, threatening to choke him.

Elizabeth stepped outside in her stocking feet and shut the door behind her. Communicating without words, they fell into each other's arms. Holding Elizabeth close, Todd sighed deeply, as if he'd been holding his breath ever since she had left the hospital with Jessica. A flood of emotions rushed through him, feelings he'd kept dammed up for so long. He felt as if he were drowning.

His control shattered. Tears poured down his face. For what seemed like forever, he and Elizabeth held each other and rocked back and forth, both of them sobbing.

Finally when the worst of the storm had passed, Todd drew in a shaky breath. "I tried to stop it," he said. He kissed Elizabeth's forehead.

"I know you did, Todd. I'm sorry I didn't have enough faith in you to tell you about Rosie's plan. Then this whole thing wouldn't have—" She started to cry again.

Todd wrapped his arms tighter around her, wishing that holding her were enough to make things better. "Please don't blame yourself," he said. "I didn't exactly give you a million reasons to trust me. The truth is I've been a jerk lately. I can't begin to tell you how sorry I am. If you forgive me, I promise I'll spend the rest of my life making it up to you."

She kissed his neck. "I need you to forgive me, too."

"Oh, of course I do." He bent down and kissed her gently. "We can start over," he whispered against her lips. He leaned back and looked into her eyes. They sparkled in the dim moonlight. "I know we can," he said. "We have to get past this, Liz."

She nodded. "You're right. What happened can't be undone. We've got to be strong and united for Jessica. She's going to need us now more than ever."

"How is she?"

Elizabeth shook her head. "I can't really tell." She sat down on the cement step and scooted over to make room for him beside her. "She's just sitting out on the back patio, staring into space. My mother tried talking to her earlier, but Jessica seems to be sinking into a cloud of despair. I'm worried about her."

"I know you are," Todd said.

"This was such a horrible accident."

Todd rested his arm across her shoulders. "But it wasn't an accident, Liz. The Palisades High guys went to Bruce's house looking for a fight. All of them have been charged with criminal trespassing. The guy who kicked Christian right before he hit his head and fell into the pool might be charged with involuntary manslaughter."

Elizabeth raised her eyebrows at that. "I hope the SVH guys aren't celebrating over it."

"Are you kidding? Everyone is pretty shaken up about all this. Even Bruce has finally come to realize that it could easily have been any one of us fac-

171

ing that manslaughter charge. No, you don't have to worry about the Sweet Valley High School gang anymore. We've disbanded permanently."

Elizabeth rested her head on his shoulder and wrapped her arms around his waist. "I'm so relieved about that, Todd. Now I just have to figure out a way to help Jessica. She seems so withdrawn and I don't know how to reach her."

They sat there for a while longer, gazing up at the stars. Sitting quietly next to Elizabeth, Todd felt the peacefulness of the night sink deep into his heart. It was a great relief finally to have his priorities straight. He vowed never to let anything come between him and Elizabeth again.

After Todd left, Elizabeth tiptoed back into the house so as not to wake her parents. Despite the late hour, going to bed was out of the question for her. She couldn't leave Jessica out on the patio alone.

Elizabeth went into the kitchen and busied herself with the task of making coffee because she didn't know what else to do. As she waited for the pot to finish dripping, she looked out the window at her sister. Jessica was huddled in a lounge chair, where she'd been for hours. She lay there so still, Elizabeth suspected she'd fallen asleep.

Careful not to wake her if she had, Elizabeth slowly opened the sliding doors and stepped outside. She crept around the patio table to the lounge chair on the other side. Jessica's eyes were wide open as she turned to Elizabeth with a blank stare.

"Hi," Elizabeth said softly. "I was just checking to see if you were sleeping."

Jessica looked right through Elizabeth as if she were transparent. "I can't figure it out," Jessica began. "One minute they were talking, the next minute they were fighting, and then . . . Christian was gone. And the fighting stopped. How could something so devastating happen in such a short span of time? It doesn't make sense."

Elizabeth sat on a corner of the chair, settling herself next to Jessica's feet. "I know it doesn't."

"He's really gone, huh?"

Elizabeth looked at her sadly and nodded. Jessica touched the coral necklace she wore. "He gave me this today, right before he told me that he'll love me forever." Her voice trembled but her eyes were dry, as if she had run out of tears.

It broke Elizabeth's heart to see Jessica so hurt and vulnerable. She wished there was something she could say to make everything better, to erase all of her sister's pain. But Elizabeth had no words of comfort. There was nothing that could ease away the grim truth of Jessica's loss.

All Elizabeth could do was hug her sister and hope that time would heal her grief.

Two weeks after Christian's death, an unexpected visitor called on Jessica. It was Saturday afternoon and she'd been lying in bed all day, where she'd spent most of her time for the past couple of weeks. Sleeping and lounging recently had become her favorite pastimes, having taken the place of cheerleading, shopping, concerts, parties, the beach, and hanging out with all of her friends. Her life seemed to have lost all meaning. She could hardly remember what it felt like to be happy and carefree. If she hadn't been forced to attend school, Jessica would never have gotten out of her bed at all.

Jessica's room suited her just fine. It was cozy and sheltered. She loved the bold color scheme of deep purple which covered the walls, the floor, and the bed. Elizabeth once said it looked as if someone had hosed everything down with grape juice, but what did she know? Jessica would have gone crazy by now if she had to live in her sister's pastels and pristine neatness. Jessica's floor was hardly visible. As was typical for her room, discarded clothing, school books, cosmetics, and magazines were strewn across the carpet in every direction.

She glanced at the bright orange envelope that was perched on top of a pile of sweaters in the corner. It had arrived in yesterday's mail with her name neatly typed on the front in capital letters.

174

She didn't have to open it to know what it was; the return address gave it away. It was the confirmation of her entry to the Rock TV all-state surfing competition. Apparently they hadn't heard that the old Jessica who cared about such things had vanished.

She rolled over and punched the pillow. *Lying in bed is a great hobby*, she thought. Not too exciting, of course. But she'd discovered, quite by accident, that when she lay perfectly still and stared at the ceiling, her insides would feel almost numb. It was the only relief she'd found so far from the wrenching pain of losing Christian.

When the doorbell rang, Jessica automatically burrowed under her purple bedspread. *If that's Lila, Amy, or anyone else with another invitation to the movies, the mall, or the Dairi Burger, I'll scream!* she thought. For the past week, Jessica had been bombarded with calls and visits from friends urging her to "get out of the house." Sure enough, Elizabeth called her name.

"Tell whoever it is to go away!" she shouted back.

Elizabeth called her again. Jessica exhaled with a strong huff. Her sister was relentless when she got her mind set on something. Jessica was sick and tired of everyone trying to cheer her up all the time. *Why can't they just give it a rest?* All she wanted was to be left alone.

Elizabeth's footsteps came up the stairs and

stopped in the hall outside Jessica's room. "Jessica?" Elizabeth tapped softly on her door. "Jessica, are you awake?"

With an angry groan, Jessica pushed aside the covers and jumped to her feet. Elizabeth opened the door and popped her head inside. Her bright smile made Jessica feel even more snarly than she already did.

"There's someone here to see you," Elizabeth said.

"I figured that," Jessica grumbled.

"It's—"

"I don't care who it is." Jessica stormed past her without bothering with a robe. Wearing a short blue nightshirt and her hair in frightening disarray, she stomped downstairs prepared to do battle with the intruder. "Okay, I'm going to say this for the last time. I don't want to go, see, do, eat, or buy anything, so why don't you just—" She stopped short, swallowing back the remainder of her sentence.

An unfamiliar woman, who looked to be in her mid-fifties, was sitting on the living-room couch, watching her with a guarded expression. She was the perfect picture of refinement in an elegant raw silk suit, which Jessica recognized as a Giordano Cora original design. It was tastefully accessorized with a double-strand necklace of black pearls, a diamond-studded gold Rolex watch, and a diamond ring large enough to use as a paperweight.

Jessica exhaled, feeling deflated and quite foolish. "I'm sorry. I thought you were someone else."

Elizabeth came up behind her, and flashing Jessica a pointed look of reproach, turned to the woman. "Dr. Gorman, may I introduce my sweet, gracious twin sister, Jessica. Jessica, this is Dr. Gorman, Christian's mother."

Jessica raised her hand to her mouth, her eyes wide. "Oh, I'm so sorry. I mean, I had no idea . . ."

The corners of Dr. Gorman's lips twitched slightly into a concealed smile. The small movement tugged at Jessica's heart. It was something she'd seen Christian do many times.

"It's a pleasure to meet you at last, Jessica," the woman said.

Jessica clapped her hands together. "I'll be right back." She turned around and began to retrace her steps to her room. Over her shoulder she said, "Elizabeth, make some tea or something. I'll just be a minute."

Once inside her room, she spun into action. The inertia she'd felt a moment ago melted off like a thin shell of ice. It had been a long time since she actually wanted a visitor. She whipped through her dresser drawers, grabbing her last clean pair of decent-looking shorts and a green tank top. With lightning speed, she ran into the bathroom which she shared with Elizabeth and took the fastest shower of her life.

Less than fifteen minutes later, a decent facsimile of the old Jessica descended the stairs and entered the living room. She'd twisted her hair into a stylish chignon at the back of her neck and applied enough makeup to cover the haggard shadows under her eyes.

When she returned to the living room, Elizabeth had laid out a plate of oatmeal cookies, napkins, a crystal pitcher of iced lemonade and two tall glasses on the marble table. Jessica smiled gratefully at her, then turned to Dr. Gorman. "I'm sorry about that, before. I'm not usually so, um—"

Elizabeth raised her eyebrows. "Spontaneous?" she interjected.

Dr. Gorman waved her hand as if to brush away Jessica's apology. "It's quite all right, dear." The expression in her eyes softened. Jessica noticed they were the exact shade of smoky blue as Christian's. "These last few weeks have been—" She took a deep breath and dabbed at the moisture in her eyes with a paper napkin.

Elizabeth stood up and poured lemonade into the glasses. "It was very nice meeting you, Dr. Gorman," she said as she set the pitcher back down on the coffee table.

"Are you leaving?" Jessica said.

"Todd's picking me up in a few minutes. I'll wait for him outside."

Jessica understood the gesture was calculated to give her and Christian's mother some privacy, but Jessica wasn't sure she wanted it. She watched Elizabeth go, then turned back to Dr. Gorman. Their eyes met and Jessica suddenly felt shy and tongue-tied. Absently she fumbled with the necklace she was wearing, taking comfort in the sensation of her fingers rubbing across the smooth ridges of coral.

Dr. Gorman's gaze followed the small movement. She smiled sadly. "Christian wore that all the time."

Jessica nodded. "I haven't taken it off since he gave it to me."

An awkward silence hung between them. Jessica caught her bottom lip between her teeth and tried to think of something to say. Dr. Gorman picked up a cookie and nibbled the edge. "These are very good. Homemade?"

"I suppose," Jessica replied.

Just then, a beeper went off. Dr. Gorman reached into the pocket of her jacket and shut off the pager. "Excuse me, Jessica. May I use your phone?"

"Of course," Jessica replied. She led Dr. Gorman to the phone in the upstairs hall and went back to the living room.

Dr. Gorman returned a few minutes later. "I'm

sorry about that," she said. "Sometimes I feel as though I'm on a leash. That blasted thing seems to go off at the worst moments. When Christian was little, he used to sneak into my study and hide it. I guess he resented the fact that every time it beeped, his mommy would disappear." A shadow of pain seemed to pass over her features.

Jessica clasped her hands tightly on her lap and said nothing. Christian was gone. It wasn't her place to tell his mother that he had felt as though he could never measure up to her expectations.

"Christian was quite a character," Dr. Gorman said. "He once managed to break into the school's computer system. Then he figured out a way to inject a virus into the system which would transpose students' grades so that every time a teacher entered an 'A' it would change to an 'F' and vice versa. I still can't believe it. He was only in seventh grade." She chuckled wistfully. "Needless to say, he caused a lot of consternation among students and faculty before he was caught."

A pain squeezed at Jessica's heart. It hurt to think of all the details about Christian that she'd never have a chance to learn. *He's gone forever,* her mind screamed. She wanted to run back upstairs and hide in her purple cell.

Dr. Gorman raised the crumpled napkin to her

eyes again. "I understand you and Christian were very good friends."

"We were in love," Jessica said succinctly.

Dr. Gorman smiled. "He seemed so happy those last few weeks. I hadn't seen him so cheerful and talkative since he was a young child. I only wish I had taken the time to listen to him," she added sadly.

"I was very happy, too," Jessica said.

"Some of his friends told me he was teaching you how to surf."

Jessica nodded, tears gathering in her eyes.

"There's a reason why I came here today," Dr. Gorman said, her tone businesslike now. She leaned forward and picked up her glass. "Besides wanting to satisfy my curiosity about the girl who stole my son's heart, of course." She stared at Jessica over the rim of her glass for a long moment. Jessica felt as if she were being tested and evaluated to her very core.

Dr. Gorman took a dainty sip of lemonade and set her glass down on the coffee table. "I've brought you something," she said, running her finger absently over the beaded moisture condensing on the glass. "It's outside." She stood up and motioned for Jessica to accompany her.

Jessica's curiosity was piqued as she followed her out the front door. Then she saw it. Propped up against Dr. Gorman's silver grey LTD was Christian's surfboard. Its yellow and turquoise markings seemed to touch her heart with their cheery brightness. In a single moment, as she stared at it, she relived all the joyous hours she'd shared with Christian. She could almost see him on it, his arms spread wide as he flew across the face of a wave. She remembered the thrilling sensation of tandem surfing on that board, with the wind in her face and Christian holding her. She didn't think she'd ever have the heart to go surfing again without him.

Tears rolled down Jessica's face as she turned to Christian's mother. Dr. Gorman sniffed. "I think Christian would have wanted you to have it, Jessica."

Epilogue

Jessica felt completely numb when she arrived at Moon Beach on the morning of the surfing competition. The sky was gray and cloudy, which matched her mood. She hardly remembered why she had wanted to enter and win so badly. Nor did it matter that everyone at Sweet Valley High had been talking about the competition all week. The only reason she had shown up at all was that she knew Christian would have wanted it.

Although the competition wasn't scheduled to begin for another hour, the beach was already crowded with spectators and surfers. A bandstand and bleachers had been set up in the sand, decorated with colorful banners advertising the various sponsors of the day's event. A van bearing the logo of Rock TV was parked alongside the bandstand,

183

and a team of roadies were setting up equipment in preparation of the opening band. Venders roamed the crowd, hawking balloons, souvenirs, and snacks.

But the carnival atmosphere was completely lost on Jessica. She couldn't help but think how exciting all this would be if Christian were with her now.

She unloaded the surfboard from the back of the Jeep, handling it with reverence. Christian's board felt like an old friend. It seemed fitting that she ride it for the competition. Since Dr. Gorman had given it to her, Jessica had kept it in her room, propped against the wall directly across from her bed, where she'd see it first thing in the morning and last thing at night. Sometimes when nightmares and painful memories kept her awake, she'd sit with her arms wrapped around Christian's board and pretend that it understood and shared her loss.

Jessica had thought her surfing days were over after Christian died. But every time she'd look at his surfboard, she'd feel a bittersweet longing. Then, a few weeks ago, she had driven to their special little beach and had ventured into the water alone. The glorious thrill of flying across the ocean had returned. It had felt right for her to be there. Surfing was what brought her and Christian together and for him, she would go on.

She hoisted the board up over her head and slammed the Jeep shut. She made her way to the Moon Beach Surf Club to sign in for the competition, taking care to step around the sunbathers lying on blankets and surfers waxing their boards on the beach.

A few people waved to her from the bleachers. She clasped the board steady with one hand and waved back. Elizabeth was sitting with Todd, Enid, Marla, and Caitlin. Jessica noticed that both Sweet Valley High and Palisades High were well represented in the crowd.

In the club house, the tension was high. Jessica stood in line, listening to the buzzing conversations around her.

"I don't remember the last time we had waves this high," the guy in back of her was saying. "I swear they're twelve feet."

"There's a good swell coming in from a storm up north," another said. "The wave length isn't too bad, but it's going to be a fast ride."

"I heard over twenty percent of the people who entered have dropped out just today," a woman behind them commented.

"Guess it's only us crazy folks left," the first guy said with a nervous laugh.

Jessica remained detached from everything going on around her. She gave her name to the contest official when it was her turn in line and took the bright yellow contest jersey he handed to her. "You're number thirty-seven," he said. "Hope it brings you luck."

Jessica nodded politely and left. Outside, she slipped the jersey over her green-and-black wet suit, which had been a gift from Elizabeth.

As Jessica walked over to the bleachers, Lila and Amy came up to her. "Are you going to make me go to school with hot pink oxide on my nose?" Lila asked with a weak smile.

The question threw Jessica off guard. For a moment she couldn't figure what Lila meant. Then she remembered the bet they'd made when Jessica first announced that she was going to win this surfing competition. Lila had laughed and said she'd go to school with hot pink oxide on her nose if Jessica won. Jessica had promised to wear a fluorescent green wet suit to school if she lost.

Although it wasn't so long ago, it seemed like ages had passed since that day when she, Lila, and Amy had strolled along the beach, checking out the cute guys. It was back before she'd met Christian, Jessica sadly realized. "Of course," Jessica said softly. "A bet's a bet."

Lila glanced over Jessica's shoulder. "Beat her anyway," she said.

Jessica looked behind her and saw Rosie Shaw

186

standing there with her Palisades High posse, glaring back at her. Something deep inside Jessica began to stir.

Elizabeth ran up to her. "Good luck, Jess," she said, giving her a quick hug. "We'll be keeping our fingers crossed."

"I don't think your fingers crossed or uncrossed are going to matter much when Jessica gets out there," Amy said, gesturing toward the water. "Those waves look like mountains. I'm surprised they aren't calling off the competition."

Lila turned to her with a wry smile. "They only do that if the waves are too small."

Jessica sat with Lila and Amy on Lila's Persian rug as they waited for the competition to begin. Lila and Amy worked on their suntans while Jessica waxed her surfboard. She felt amazingly calm.

Amy held out a plastic tube. "Want some suntan oil, Jessica?"

"Give me that," Lila said, grabbing it away from Amy. "Surfers can't use suntan oil, silly girl. They'll slip off their boards."

Amy shrugged. "Sorry, I didn't know." She lowered her head, using her folded arms as a pillow. "Wake me up when it starts."

A few of the PH guys came over to say hi and wish Jessica good luck. Their conversation was awkward, but nevertheless she appreciated the gesture. Jessica looked around and noticed that, except for Rosie and her friends, everyone from SVH and PH was making an effort to be friendly to one another. The two groups weren't exactly gushing with brotherly love, but it seemed everyone wanted to forget the rivalry as quickly as possible.

When the time came for the competition to begin, Tina Terrell of Rock TV climbed up onto the bandstand and ran to center stage. She was wearing a royal blue miniskirt and black half top with the Rock TV logo emblazed across her chest. "Welcome to the first annual Rock TV all-state surfing competition," she called, her voice echoing over the powerful sound system. "We're coming to you live from—" she glanced upward and wrinkled her nose at the camera— "not-so-sunny Southern California, where more than one hundred and sixty surfers are getting ready to compete for the fabulous prize of an all-expense-paid dream vacation to Hawaii, also known among these people as surf-heaven, and an exclusive interview on Rock TV. The ocean is really churning out there, as you can see behind me. Those waves are over ten feet high!

"There's a lot of excitement here today. *Lyve Deth* will be joining us later with songs from their new CD, and much more. So stay tuned to Rock TV."

After a smattering of applause, the competition

was officially opened. An athletic-looking woman wearing a black wet suit with blue piping took the stage and explained the rules. The surfers would compete in groups of twelve in the preliminary round. Each contestant was allowed to take up to ten rides in their allotted time, but only the three best rides would be counted for judging purposes. "Time will be signaled like this—" She held a horn up to the microphone and compressed it. The woman went on to explain the requirements for making it to the semifinals and finals, which would be held in the afternoon. Jessica stopped listening. She was staring at the waves, feeling lost. Making it through the preliminary round might require a miracle, she thought. She'd never surfed in waves that high.

Jessica and Rosie Shaw were assigned to the same group. A dozen women lined up on the shore, facing the water. When the signal was given, Jessica followed Rosie into the water. She'd never surfed in a crowd before and seeing the other women paddling on either side of her was distracting. She didn't feel prepared, hadn't practiced enough. Everything she'd learned under Christian's guidance flew out of her head. She had no idea how to go about surfing. She could barely remember how to swim. *This is crazy*, Jessica thought. She seriously considered turning around.

Just then, Rosie turned to her with a menacing,

sarcastic smile. "Last chance to save yourself, cheerleader," she said.

That's it, Jessica said to herself. *I'll show her!* There was no turning back. Jessica was going to win this competition—or drown in the process.

As she paddled out, Jessica felt stronger and stronger. The red and turquoise stripes on Christian's board glistened under the veil of water washing over it. She felt as if he were there with her, adding his strength to her own.

She tucked her fears away and studied the approaching waves. Recalling Christian's instruction on how to judge the best point for takeoff, Jessica picked a promising wave. As she stood up on the board, she felt the adrenaline pumping through her body. The familiar excitement of being chased by a mountain of water drove away every other thought. She managed to complete seven rides before the horn sounded again, signaling the end of the heat. Feeling exhausted, she lay down on the surfboard and rode it back to shore. *I did my best*, she mused. Christian would have been proud of that.

"That was a nice try, honey," Rosie taunted, "but you're so far out of your league it's not even funny."

Jessica stuck her tongue out at her. Then, feeling immensely satisfied, Jessica turned away and ignored Rosie for the rest of the ride to shore.

The beach was crowded. Jessica nearly collided with an elderly man carrying a cardboard tray of hot dogs. She carried her surfboard over to Lila and Amy and plopped down on the rug. "I'm beat!"

"Here, have a soda," Amy said, pulling out a cold can from her cooler.

"Be quiet," Lila said. "They're getting ready to announce the people who made it to the semifinals."

Jessica held her breath. Rosie Shaw had received the highest score in the preliminary round, so hers was the first name called. As each subsequent semifinalist was announced, Jessica was certain her name would be next. But when Tina Terrell reached the twenty-fifth name, it wasn't "Jessica Wakefield."

"Oh, well, better luck next time," Lila said.

"It's amazing that you made it even this far," Amy said.

Just then, Tina Terrell's voice came back over the speakers. "Excuse me, I have an announcement to make. One of the semifinalists in the women's division has dropped out. Taking her place will be the surfer with the twenty-sixth highest score in the preliminary round. And that is . . ." She looked down and scanned the paper in her hand. "Jessica Wakefield. Congratulations to our semifinalists and good luck this afternoon."

Elizabeth came running over to her. "Jessica, this is great."

Jessica exhaled a deep breath. "I don't know if I'm ready to face those waves again."

"You'll do fine," Elizabeth said, patting her shoulder.

Lila and Amy invited Jessica to have lunch with them at the nearby Moon Beach cafe, but she was too nervous to eat. She settled for a glass of orange juice from the snack bar instead.

As Jessica was standing at the counter, she heard Rosie's voice behind her. Jessica turned and looked, but Rosie hadn't noticed her.

"The preliminary round is to weed out the obvious kooks and losers who can't float at all," Rosie was saying to her friends. "The semifinals and final rounds are where the real surfing begins. The judges are looking for functional moves— skillful trimming, turning, good takeoffs. That little cheerleader isn't going to get anywhere. I was watching her. She has good balance and can stand up, but big deal. She's too scared to do anything that counts."

Jessica felt her blood steaming. She slammed down the money to pay for her orange juice and dug her toe in the sand impatiently as she waited for the clerk to ring up the sale. Then she stomped over to Rosie. "Sounds to me like you have this whole competition figured out," Jessica said in a voice dripping with sarcasm.

"Not really," Rosie answered. "There are a few girls out there who might give me a run for my money. But you—" She looked Jessica up and down. "—you're not one of them."

"We'll just see about that."

"Yes," Rosie said with a sneer, "we will. After today, you'll gladly go back to your little skirt and pom-poms."

Jessica stormed off, their cackling laughter ringing in her ears. *We'll just see if you're laughing when this is over*, she thought hotly.

The semifinals eliminated twenty more contestants. To Jessica's surprise, her rage at Rosie had given her the edge she needed to place among the five female surfers in the final round.

Rosie's criticism reverberated in Jessica's mind as she paddled out with the other finalists. She had been playing it safe so far, working as hard as she could just to avoid wiping out. But in order to win, she knew she'd have to let go.

The waves seemed to be coming faster. Jessica wondered how she was supposed to let go when they loomed so high and menacing. She glanced to her side and saw Rosie a few yards away, already up on her board, whipping across the water as if it were the most natural thing in the world.

"I'm going to do it," Jessica whispered as she pulled herself up to her feet. She shifted her weight to position the board directly parallel to the line of the wave and moved in as close as she could for maximum speed, a maneuver called "trimming" which Christian had demonstrated many times. Flying across the face of the wave faster than ever before, she took a deep breath and executed a series of perfect three-hundred-sixty degree turns, ending up in the same direction in which she'd started.

Suddenly the lip of the wave began to curl down over her until she was completely encased deep in the hollow tube of the wave. The frightening sound of churning water roared in her ears. It was as if she were caught in a giant blender, about to be pureed. The only other time this had happened to her, she'd nearly drowned. Christian had saved her then. But now, her only hope was to stay up on the board until she came out the other end.

Jessica's heart banged against her chest. She was engulfed in her own fear, as heavy as a cement jacket. Her foot slipped and she over-compensated with her arms. The board started to wobble under her feet. Jessica realized she was losing her balance.

Don't panic, her mind screamed. She prepared herself for a controlled wipeout, mentally running down the list of things Christian had taught her: stay relaxed, hold the board if possible, let the water help her to the surface, then check the position of the next wave. She could almost hear his voice whispering each point in her ear.

Suddenly a deep calm filled her. The board became steady and she regained her balance. She stopped thinking about the techniques, about anything. With a surge of joy, she let herself ride free. She felt as if she had merged with the ocean and its power became hers. Her natural rhythm carried her along and with astonishing skill, she shot the curl and completed the ride victoriously.

Elizabeth felt as if her heart was about to burst with pride as she watched her twin sister from the shore. Jessica looked triumphant, riding the waves with grace, style, and power, as though she'd taken control of the sea. Now she understood what Jessica meant when she'd spoken of the special times she'd shared surfing with Christian.

Elizabeth remembered when she had taken surfing lessons herself and had entered a surfing competition here at Moon Beach. She'd done it to prove that she wasn't the stodgy old Elizabeth everyone thought she was. Whether she'd succeeded in proving anything, she wasn't sure. She had enjoyed the experience tremendously, although she was nowhere near to matching Jessica's incredible skill.

Caitlin and Marla were sitting with Elizabeth and Todd, gaping at Jessica. "Your sister is something else," Marla said.

"She's fabulous," Caitlin said.

"Yeah, she is," Elizabeth readily agreed. She could almost feel the joy radiating from Jessica's smile. Under her breath, Elizabeth whispered a thanks to Christian, wherever he was, for giving her sister such a wonderful gift.

Jessica carried her board to shore, her body exhausted, but her spirits soaring. People rushed over to her, surrounding her, patting her on the back, cheering. She looked around in awe, as though she was surprised to see everyone there.

Someone wrapped a towel around her. Then Elizabeth hugged her, chanting, "You did it, you did it!"

"I guess it's a hot pink nose for me," Lila said.

"You were great," Todd said.

To Jessica's surprise, Rosie came over and stoically shook her hand. Then someone placed a huge trophy in Jessica's arms and Tina Terrell stuck a microphone in her face. Everyone was clapping.

Staring at the trophy, Jessica realized that she'd won. "I did it," she murmured. She looked up and smiled brightly. "I did it!"

She felt alive. For the first time since Christian hit his head, she felt like a real human being—sort of.

Christian's faith in her and the memory of their love had given her the strength to win today. She knew his memory would always be there to help her face the future.

Hugging his surfboard to her side, Jessica looked straight into the camera and leaned toward the mike. "I won this for Christian Gorman," she said, holding up the trophy. "The bravest man I ever knew."

As the crowd cheered, the sun broke through the clouds.

How far will Jessica go to stop a gorgeous ski instructor from falling into Lila Fowler's clutches? Will Elizabeth manage to rescue Todd Wilkins after he's buried in an avalanche? Find out during an unforgettable ski vacation with the SVH gang on the slopes of Colorado in **Falling for Lucas,** *a new Sweet Valley High Super Edition!*

Bantam Books in the Sweet Valley High series
Ask your bookseller for the books you have missed

SIGN UP FOR THE SWEET VALLEY HIGH® FAN CLUB!

Hey, girls! Get all the gossip on Sweet Valley High's® most popular teenagers when you join our fantastic Fan Club! As a member, you'll get all of this really cool stuff:

- Membership Card with your own personal Fan Club ID number
- A Sweet Valley High® Secret Treasure Box
- Sweet Valley High® Stationery
- Official Fan Club Pencil (for secret note writing!)
- Three Bookmarks
- A "Members Only" Door Hanger
- Two Skeins of J. & P. Coats® Embroidery Floss with flower barrette instruction leaflet
- Two editions of *The Oracle* newsletter
- Plus exclusive Sweet Valley High® product offers, special savings, contests, and much more!